NO NAME KEY

No Name Key

JESSICA ARGYLE

MACLAWRAN

Key West

Copyright © 2014 Jessica Argyle

All Rights Reserved.

Published by Maclawran
maclawran.com

ISBN-13: 978-1-4960-5559-0
ISBN-10: 1496055594

FIRST EDITION

Book design by Sean MacGuire,
Cover painting by Jessica Argyle
Edited by Laurie Skemp

Printed in the USA

*For Sean, my husband, who loves
me almost as much as I love him*

"*In your life there are a few places, or maybe only the one place, where something happened, and then there are all the other places.*"

— Alice Munro, *Too Much Happiness*

NO NAME KEY

PROLOGUE

Less than two weeks at the work camp and Billy Woodman was up to his old tricks, drunkenly cursing her and accusing her of lying with his boss. Next morning she pretended to be asleep inside the narrow sleep sack when the highway crew manager took him outside to tell him his days were numbered if he didn't straighten up, that "many more are willing to take your place." He lowered his voice, but Elle could still hear him. "And, no place for a woman," he added, and she knew it was true.

This Hooverville at Matecumbe Key was situated a scant 30 miles south of Miami, Florida, and housed 600 vets, of the so-called Great War. By the time they arrived, many were crazed from the ill treatment received at the hands of a government that no longer wished to acknowledge any debt for their service. They were amongst the most vulnerable victims of what Hoover termed "a great depression" and were finally offered a job building roads in the sun, for a dollar a day. Medical care, meals and housing came with the deal; if you could call food fit for dogs and a flimsy tent a home. Few rules applied, but the most important was that if the men didn't work, they wouldn't be paid.

Elle saw any chance to work as a gift, and this offer came just in time, for they were practically homeless, living on the grudging largesse of Elle's Uncle George, who made no bones about his desire to see the backs of both her and Billy Woodman.

But Billy refused to leave without her, so the two of them made their way from Boston to join a road crew in the steamy swampland of south Florida. The ambitious plan was to string a pearl necklace out of the fragile 120-mile stretch of broken land called the Florida Keys, allowing rich men to drive their shiny cars on an uninterrupted road to Key West. But to the vets doing the work, it had come to seem more like a way to have the old soldiers disappear altogether.

After twelve hard years of marriage to Billy Woodman, Elle was all out of pity for her husband and was tired of endlessly shoring him up. *I got him here, settled him in, and now it's time for me to be off. Just like I planned.*

That morning the camp boss finally delivered the letter she had mailed to herself before leaving Boston. She wiped her hands on her thin cotton dress, fearful that Billy would know the letter for what it was: a sham and a fake.

"Here," she said. "You open it."

Billy sat on the thin cot, his chest bare and dark, muscles knotted from swinging an anvil in the sun. His temple pulsated.

"Never got no good tidings in a letter," he said. "You read it." He threw it toward where she crouched on the cot. She opened it as casually as she could muster then straightened her spine to read it aloud.

February 15, 1935
Boston, Massachusetts

Dear Mr. and Mrs. Woodman,

As discussed with Mrs. Woodman's uncle, George O'Neil, I am pleased to extend an offer to Mrs. Woodman for the position of lady's maid to my widowed daughter, Edna Benson, and her three children. This position will include duties as general helper and cook. We know and believe Elle Woodman to be of good moral character and a steady worker, but we regret that we have room only for her for the first six months. After such time, if all is amenable, we will happily take on Mr. Billy Woodman as mechanic and family chauffeur.

Further, we will reimburse y`ou for the fare and incidentals and have Mrs. Woodman share a room with baby Winifred. If Mrs. Woodman does not arrive within the coming two weeks, we will assume that you have declined and the offer will be rescinded.

In Good Faith,
Frederick Benson

"It's the times, Billy. They're calling it a great depression now and we have to take what we can get."

Elle wondered where she conjured up the only scenario that might get her away from him. "Oh, Billy. It's what you wanted…to work with cars," Elle said, knowing that was the only good news to him.

"Not like this, Elle." He ground his teeth.

And later, "Gee, Billy, it's got to be better than here." She shooed away a blood-heavy mosquito as it veered unsteadily toward the thin tent wall. "It's a fresh start, that's what it is."

Billy rose and slapped the insect and blood splattered in the air, landing in a fine spray on her feet. She was amazed at how much they could hold.

"You…a common servant. I only want you to serve me, Elle. It's not right."

By next morning, he had weakened, and she knew she had only a sliver of time to grab her chance and get away from him.

"Don't you see, Billy, our fortunes have changed. First you found work, now me. Soon you get to do what you really want. Maybe someday you'll have a business of your own."

"Billy," she said later, with a gentleness she no longer felt. "Tomorrow is the day. If I don't get a move on, the only job I been offered in the past year will be lost." She took both his hands in hers, "With me saving all I make and what you will get, we can put up stakes someplace of our own." She lied, then made herself small, never knowing what would set him off.

That night she endured his rage as he moved between anger, desire and self-pity, making enough noise to mark her as his in the wee hours, making sure all of Hooverville heard her cries.

After he had his eggs and left with the crew, she packed quickly and trekked as fast as the rubble and muck in the road would allow. She had left him a note promising to write when she arrived in Boston. But Elle had no intention of ever returning to the home of her youth. The home where her parents had died and her uncle had suffered her keep, his obvious relief visible when she introduced him to Billy Woodman, who had come a-courting. It would have made no difference if the man had two heads and spit teeth, anything to be rid of her.

She finally arrived at the ferry landing where a large northbound boat was docked. Hooverville was still visible from the landing, though all seemed to do their best to pretend they didn't see the tents looming on the horizon, like sickly pustules. *Good riddance.*

When she arrived in Miami, she would hop a bus to the Carolinas. It didn't matter to Elle that she had no plan beyond that. She was free.

I

Elle was drawn in by shrieks of laughter and music blaring from the other side of the large wharf. *How odd,* she thought, *the music seems to be cranked in from automobiles.* The airy and happy sound drew her to a smaller ferry called *The Key Wester.* People on board this vessel looked struck by fairy dust, as polished and shiny as their buffed bright cars. A curly-haired tot in a sailor suit, as sweet a boy as the murdered Lindbergh baby, smiled at her, and a man who looked to be the First Mate yelled down.

"You with the family, ma'am? Getting ready to depart. We do our best to stay on schedule."

"To Key West?" she replied stupidly.

He looked at her curiously.

Could she manage it? Did she dare?

"Yes, I'm with the family," she said motioning in the general direction of the forty or so passengers, many with small children.

"Don't let me hold you up," he said with a wink. "Mr. Monty at your service." With that, he held out his hand, yanked her up with surprising force, and within a few minutes they were on the move. Not ten minutes into the trip he returned, wearing white gloves and tilting an engraved silver tray under her nose.

"Miss. Would you care for a snack?" Sandwiches, all wrapped neatly in frilly white paper crowded the tray. She was about to reach for one when she saw the sign marked 15 cents. She shook her head at the dapper First Mate.

"G'wan, miss, it's on the company."

"Not looking for any handout. No sir."

"Suit yourself. Told you my name, what's yours?"

"Mrs. ..." But then she stopped. "My name is Elle."

Despite rumors that Key West was in decline, with thousands of jobs lost and uncollected garbage festering on the streets because the city was bankrupt, she wanted to see for herself. She had grown up on tales of Key West, one of the wealthiest cities in America — a storied and odd Southern port city where she just might find a situation to sustain her. If she couldn't, she would move on to the Carolinas as she originally planned.

Anything was better than returning to freezing, cold Boston, as inhospitable to a woman on the run from her man as anywhere she could imagine. Besides, Billy would never think she would head further south.

A stiffly coiffed older woman spotted her, opened her mouth to speak, but after taking another long, hard look at her, she turned away as if Elle was no longer there. Elle's obvious poverty protected her from a lingering gaze. The last thing this gang fancied was another sob sister tale, this time from the despairing wife of a war veteran working the highway project.

Monty smiled at her from the other side of the boat, and Elle straightened her tall body as if to warn him off. But soon she thought better of making a spectacle of herself and made herself as invisible as possible in this oversized tub ferrying the cars of some of the wealthiest people she had ever laid eyes on. Feeling like a ragamuffin, even in her best outfit of navy serge, she hoped to pass herself off as a servant to one of the families in the shiny Packards or Fords. Cars were parked heel to toe while their owners' happy talk danced on the air as if they had not a care in the world.

The first mate had been kind though. Even so, she made sure to get a proper stamped ticket, convinced that he would pocket her fare if he could. And who would blame him, cash being in short supply for none but the most favored, all decked out in outfits that she had only seen on the covers of certain magazines. Elle had no idea of how to approach them but figured she'd best learn, somehow certain that her fate would depend upon their approval.

The ferry bounced along, and finally Elle was hungry enough to regret that she hadn't accepted Monty's offering of a sandwich. They were just another couple of hours to Key West when Monty announced that they would be stopping at a dot on the map with the unlikely name of No Name Key.

Elle was miffed she hadn't been aware this stop was on the roster, but she blamed herself for being uninformed. As they docked, she saw a couple on deck that stood out, being far more unkempt and bedraggled than anyone on board.

An officious man, red-faced and impatient, corralled Monty, and Elle heard him say something sharp about a thief.

She put on her best smile. "Excuse me, sir, but maybe I can be of service."

"Who are you?" the large, beet-red faced man asked,

annoyed at being interrupted. Elle knew he had taken her measure, her thrifty appearance relieving him of the chore of being overly polite.

"My name is Elle Woodman, professional cook and all around helper."

He took her in. Monty stepped up.

"Yes. Just look at her—more muscle that the two of us put together, if I may be so bold."

"You looking for work? Can't pay much and taking help on in a purely probationary basis. Last pair I hired was thieves. So be warned miss—if I catch you stealing, this time I *will* call the police. Tired of it."

And so within a few short hours of leaving Billy Woodman, her fortune had begun to change.

Over the next couple of months, Elle did the work of two, and the owners only hired extra help for the weekends. She ran the show, and her long days settled into a steady rhythm. Often left to fend for herself, Elle enjoyed being master of her time. She got to know the fishermen and the iceman who stocked the icehouse, and she made bargains with the merchants that brought food to No Name Lodge.

"Got a theory on suffering," she told Jim, one of the fishermen who stopped by to fill the larder when guests were plenty.

"What is it, Elle?" he asked.

"Figure you got to suffer either way in life. Only difference is, one is from never having the gumption to take a chance, and the other from the anxiety of taking it. Choose your poison."

"Guess I have a long time to think on that," he said. She liked speaking with Jim, though he usually said little, saving it up for his invalid wife.

Spring gave way to summer and, despite the choking heat and aggressive insects, the Florida fever had her. Open water, uninhabited ribbons of land, and vivid blue skies held her in awe. She loved nothing more than standing barefoot on the wharf at sunset, alone, and free of Billy Woodman. But twice a day, when the ferry came by, she listened for signs of men from the work camps, doing her best to avoid meeting the guests until the boat departed. She knew the vets would have no cause to stop here. No, more than likely, they were looking to spend their paychecks on the charms that Key West had to offer.

In the lodge library, she ran her eyes over the spines of leather bound volumes of books looking for tales of beachcombers who set up stakes on small plots of land. Adventure tales, pirates and castaways were her favorites. On a slow day, a month into her job, Elle set out to explore the island, hoofing through the bushes, and came upon a grove of trees with odd, saucer shaped fruit. Out of the brush, a tall, thin man appeared carrying an old shotgun.

"I mean no harm, sir," she said, but she stood her ground. Best to face him square on. "These need tending."

He said nothing, so she moved toward one of the trees laden with fruit about to drop. "Almost rotten. You have help in these parts?"

"You offering?" He seemed to want to say more but speaking pained him. So she looked away from his face as one looks away from a wild animal, not knowing if it will flee, or attack. Later she found out he was a hermit, but no ordinary vagrant, though he certainly looked the part. He owned more than half of No Name Key and was as widely known for his orchards as his need for solitude. Up front, Elle asked the owners of No Name Lodge if she could help him.

"Don't mind you picking some crops for the old man, Elle. If you can make yourself a little extra, go ahead, so long as it doesn't interfere with duties around here."

But all that changed, not three months into her freedom, when Billy discovered where she was. Elle had managed to avoid meeting the ferryboat when it came in, as was her practice. She knew men from the camps took their leave in Key West when they had full pay packets, spending their few sweat-earned dollars on the pleasures the town offered. And she was sure it was just a matter of time before Billy found out where she had landed.

"I got your stuff." It was him. Billy, his voice carried on a wave, and a woman's cheerful command followed it. "Well, let's go then.. Start up the engines, Billy-boy."

Billy-boy? A woman?

But she was ready for him, scrambling to the wharf, running to him before he got a word out of his mouth.

"I thought you would never come, Billy. I figure you was mad at me."

The woman in the car straightened her neck and jutted her chin out at him. Her pale blue scarf licked the perfect ball of her snow-white shoulder, then fluttered behind her in the wind. "What are you doing? Who the devil is she?"

Elle waited for Billy to speak, but he was unable to respond. He looked from Elle to the woman, and finally Elle decided to risk speaking again.

"Who is she, Billy?" She figured she should ask but was more relieved that someone else had his attention.

"Doin' work on the car for Mrs. Rowlands and her husband. Helping them out."

I'll bet you are, she thought, convinced further when the

woman, who had turned sharply away, now thought better of it and commanded Billy to help her out of the car.

A small crowd formed, sensing conflict, but pretending to look elsewhere, turning silent whenever one of them spoke.

Billy motioned Elle off to the side and, when they were more or less alone, he grabbed ahold of her by the shoulders. Elle was torn between the fear of him coming after her and the pleasure that someone as fine as that fancied up strumpet would have to fend for herself. Not accustomed to it; that much was plain.

She spoke fast, counting on his refusal to grasp the fact that she could ever survive on her own and didn't want him back. She told him a long tale of being stranded in Boston then making it back with the promise of a job in No Name Key Lodge. And to her immense relief he bought the whole story, having more to hide than she did. "Deal with all that later," he said, his eyes rubbering around the wharf, looking for his fancy lady and mumbling like the lout he was.

Old man Rowlands waved at him from the car and Elle sensed that Billy made the old man nervous and suspicious. While gathering up the crowd, she caught the woman and Billy whispering. Without incident, Billy was off on the last ferry back to Matecumbe and the work camp. But Elle knew it was only a matter of time before he would come gunning for her. She could see it in his eyes.

Billy didn't return for another month, until the peak of the summer season at the end of July. But it may as well have been the next day. The thought of Billy coming for her propelled her to scrub and polish the lodge clean and work till the wee hours making recipes more delicious with each workout. Anything to make up for the trouble she knew he would cause. When she was done, she would head out-of-doors and pick the hermits fruit with a fury, as if she could glean favor from the land and the inhabitants of No Name Key to keep her safely tucked away from Billy Woodman. She was brown and sinewy from the sun, her red hair bleached into a tangled nest—a sight that even made the hermit start when he found her working late into the evening.

Soon Billy was coming regularly to get her pay packet and head on out to Key West, sometimes with the Rowlandses. She always kept some money back, tucking it away against the tragedy that she knew had to be brewing at Billy's hands.

By August, he showed up more than once a week, knowing season would soon be upon them. But during one weekend, late in the slow season, Elle heard the slam of the owner's cabin door. When she peered out the window, she saw them, the owner in a gauze nightshirt that revealed more of him than Elle ever wished to see. He was shooing a drunken Billy away, telling him to "sleep it off." After yelling at her to open the door, Billy pissed against the side of the lodge and Elle was certain the owner must have seen him in the act.

Next morning, the owner had the same look as when he ousted the couple the day she arrived to take their place. Elle could feel the cold creeping up on her and distance growing between them. She knew she would already have been ousted from this job if she didn't do the work of three. And then, as quickly as Billy blew in, he was gone for the next two weeks. She needed to finish her small house and get him away from the lodge. Maybe she could stash him there, hiding him away from the owners and the guests of No

Name Key Lodge, when his moods lay siege to her like a tempest at sea.

2

Elle, redheaded and buxom, squinted into the horizon, taking in the bleached driftwood on the shore. Her yellow sleeves hung limp in the thick air as she stood tall in men's boots, already feeling the heat of the day and the rising temperature. It was late August and No Name Key was so deserted that she swore she could hear the damp bodies of insects hatching as warm water lapped against the spongy shore.

Dog raced out ahead of her but then stopped, cautious, as if sensing that Billy may be near. As she trudged across the newly cleared field, Elle planned her strategy, and Dog hunkered in close, as if conspiring with her. Once she got her sink, she would be well on her way to converting the concrete cistern into a proper home. Then she could make good on her promise to keep Billy away from guests of No Name Lodge.

She ran her mind over the list of chores for the fishing tournament: the stock of booze, trophy for first prize, party favors, and enough crabs for her famous chowder. Elle was more grateful than proud that her cooking and knowledge of home cures were enough to earn her keep. That, and the long workday, usually from sunup to sundown.

The ferry wasn't due for another half hour, so she slowed her pace and moved past the wall of seagrape that hid the icehouse and chicken coop from view before it opened to a widened, still unpaved pathway. *They better get to it quick*, she thought, noting that the landscape strained to claim the empty pathway, the vines and plants blurring the edges, even on the quarter mile walk to the pier.

Dog whined, then nosed her leg, making her aware that she was biting her bottom lip. Although she had begged Billy not to come for the week of the popular Labor Day Bonefish Challenge, she imagined him slinging his dusty duffel over his shoulder, trekking out of the work camp in the wee hours, cadging the four hour ferry ride from Matecumbe, through the twisted Florida Keys waterway, to No Name Key.

Revelers coming to the small island did not particularly like to be reminded of the poverty all around them, so ageing soldiers like Billy were cautioned to be on their best behavior if they expected a free ride. Lodge owners tolerated no evidence of men on the dole, even though the entire town of Key West, just thirty miles to the south, had been in dire straits for the past two years. Since 1933, breadlines looped the town so tight they just about strangled it.

But Billy enjoyed nothing more than being set loose amongst proper guests on the ferryboat. His frown softened as he zeroed in on the one sympathetic face — maybe a New Deal liberal who would nod at his sad tales — while the ferry wended its way to No Name Lodge, indifferent to the otherworldly beauty of the Florida Keys.

Once he got going, he found it impossible to stop, or so

Elle had been told. She learned of his sweet-talking ways years ago, and that's what had landed her in the mess she was in now. Only the words were different. Now he was shilling the never-ending story of the backbreaking work needed to build the 120-mile stretch of highway that would finally unite the small islands of the Florida Keys.

He made sure everyone thought that the vets worked ten hours at a shift for a dollar a day and were paid grudgingly, as if it were a handout. But it wasn't true. Regulations required that the vets never worked more than a few hours at a time and men like Billy took full advantage of the fact. *He never has a dime to spare for me, but somehow whiskey and tobacco are always plentiful*, she thought as she shook her head in disgust.

Still and all, it was not her fault when she got in the way of his anger and he couldn't find anyone else to spend it on. Billy was downright mean, even when he forgot about the mortar shots in the trenches. Elle had begun to realize that his wicked temper had nothing to do with the war, though he was quick to blame it when he could. "Waste of time thinking on Billy all the time. You know it, Dog," she said patting her big yellow dog.

Her words trailed off, interrupted by the sharp memory of the last talk with the owners. "One more scene with Billy and we'll have to let you go, Elle. Hate to do it but can't tolerate any more complaints. Sorry Elle, but this is your last warning."

Luckily, for her, guests stayed in cabins and were too busy with their own concerns to notice the problems of a lowly cook.

Dog raised his eyebrows to her then bit at the air in a futile attempt to stave off insects diving at his sturdy body.

In the distance, a freshly caught sailfish hung from a trophy rack, a timely reminder to guests that the trip was worth the trouble it took to get to this isolated spot. Even with the tropical heat at its most intense, the prestige of winning first prize in the Labor Day fishing contest brought them down in droves. Elle marveled at how a Hollywood big shot like Cecil B. DeMille needed to prove he still had moxie and had not gone as soft as the starlets on his casting couch.

Elle quickened her pace, her mind flitting from the unpicked crops to the sapodilla pie recipe she would try out on the guests, but then darkened at the thought of Billy. *Oh yes, he is coming for me, scrounging off the good-natured Captain, coming to cause me grief.*

Storm season meant hordes of hungry insects, and none but the most ardent fishermen could bear up for long under a hot Florida Keys sun that could bubble and bake the skin off your face if you weren't careful. The possibility of hurricanes added to the thrill of the chase, and Elle expected to have a full house on her hands.

After the weeklong contest was done, all would weary of the charms of the hunt, hop in their cars, and escape to points south before making their way back home. The road to Key West spanned a series of freshly built wooden bridges that crossed over narrow channels, past a kaleidoscope of blue and green water on both sides of the winding ribbon of road. "A man's trip and a rich man's paradise" was how she had heard it put, and she knew they were speaking of the well-known whorehouses. Word had it that in Key West anything could be had for a price, and a small one at that.

3

Billy's old work boots were too big, despite cloth stuffed in the toes and laces wound twice to hold the topsides to her ankles. In between airing out the sheets and setting racks of dough to rise in the warm spot by the stove, she hadn't bothered to tie her hair back properly and the heat had gotten to it bad, kinking it into a red haze that refused to lie flat.

When she reached the long pier, she stopped to flatten her hair so guests of No Name Lodge wouldn't tell tales and joke about "the crazy lady" come to greet them. Damn Monty. He was First Mate, and it was his job to see to the passengers, his reward being free lodging when he made his numbers. But he counted on her help, as if she didn't have enough to do.

A first-rate postcard artist could have designed the wharf, with its planks all gold, and oiled and even. At day's end, Elle never tired of walking to the edge of the pier to watch the sun change from pink to gold to orange then blue and purple. She never saw the same show twice. She didn't miss anything about Boston, with inky skies and a comfortless sun. She harbored not a single doubt that she was where she was meant to be.

Dog, her serious-looking yellow giant, sat next to her on the pier, fearfully staring out to sea, as if he knew Billy was on his way back to them. He had come to her as animals do, latching on for their own reasons—food and shelter mostly—till they can't be denied. He just walked out of the brush one day and she didn't inquire too deeply, thinking if anyone cared, they would have come looking for him.

She spotted the ferry in the distance then heard faint laughter and buzzing voices. The boat was full and Elle visualized the well-packed and stocked larder at the lodge. No worries there. She nosed the air as if she could tell from the smell if Billy was on board the boat.

Monty hopped out first, tipped his hat to her, shook his head from side-to-side and mouthed "no" to let her know Billy was not on the ferry. Elle smiled, grateful for his kindness, and soon the air filled with the sound of car engines starting up and music blaring from radios. They seemed to keep on coming, each fancier than the last.

When parking spots on the lodge side were full, Monty directed cars to the other side of the pier; the side belonging to the hermit. *He's not going to like it,* Elle thought, and she didn't need a frustrated hermit to add to her woes. His sapodilla trees needed picking badly or the fruit would fall and rot. Tomatoes ripened daily and were already on the verge of spoiling. It was up to her to do the bulk of the work; the hermit didn't like others meddling into his affairs. If she worked into dawn over the next couple of weeks, she would have it all packed and carted-off proper, turning a tidy profit for the hermit and enough for her to finish the roof on her property. *But why did everything have to happen at the same time? Darn this stupid tournament.*

Elle stepped up, straightening all six feet of herself, and rubbed dirt off her arms. Wouldn't do for them to see a slovenly cook.

First Mate Monty wove himself in between parked cars, opening doors, helping the women out. Thankfully, the ground was dry and hard so the polished shoes of the ladies wouldn't sink into mud. A child rubbed her eyes and squinted at the sun. It was growing hotter by the minute. One of the women slapped the child's hand. "Don't look into the sun. You'll go blind."

The men followed Monty's lead, and he soon had the group rounded up into a tidy little bundle. Elle smoothed her best yellow blouse and nodded at the women, from one to another.

Monty spoke. "This here's Elle, world famous cook over at No Name." He looked toward the lodge, all eyes following his line of vision. "Some say she invented the key lime pie and all agree that she makes the best crab chowder in the Keys. Husband works over at Matecumbe on the government road project." He took off his hat as he mentioned Billy, a habit whenever he spoke of Great War veterans.

"Pleasure," Elle said, and the woman nodded, though none held out a hand for shaking. The elder of two boys hovered around a matronly woman. *Too old to hide behind his mother's skirts,* Elle thought. When she moved the group toward the lodge, a smiling, overly made-up woman wearing bright red lipstick motioned for her to wait and walked back to speak to someone, posing, as if she were in a movie. *It was her,* Elle thought, the woman she had seen with Billy. But the woman didn't seem to notice her.

"Billy nowhere to be seen," Monty told Elle under his breath, the party preoccupied with baggage, waiting for the dolled-up woman to return.

Elle nodded. "Maybe coming in on the train." She knew she looked worried, unhappy at the prospect of his arrival. Monty could see it on her face. The whole wharf was silent, sucked in by the air. The sky had that hazy glare only present in the tropics, the sun unable to nose itself out of the misty flatness.

"Got to be patient with Billy. Bound to be angry, hungry," Monty said. "Can't blame the man for that. Work you to the bone at Matecumbe, building that everlasting road. Still though, not so bad as some other places I've seen. Pay on time, better than being on the dole."

"Much better. I try to tell him that." She pursed her lips.

"Yah, for most." He raised his eyebrows and she imagined he was referring to Billy's habit of getting handouts he didn't need.

Elle didn't nod agreement. She had learned to keep her own counsel; always better to let them talk.

Dog pawed at something he found on the pier, picked up a branch, and whimpered. "Wait," she said, hushing him with her hand as the woman with red lipstick joined the group.

"Well now, everyone, welcome to No Name Key," Monty said. "And before you ask, yes it has been called that since before 1849, they say, a favorite spot for pirates to hide their treasure. So if you see anything shiny, you'd best pocket it and keep it to yourself." He winked then launched into a brief history lesson, speaking quickly, as if it would stop them from looking around too closely, pointing out only what he wanted them to see.

The women listened while the men began looking around. Someone let out a long whistle. Elle knew what he was seeing, here for the first time—a place owned by the bugs, a place that couldn't decide if it were forest or swamp, a place where a body could drop off and out of sight if you turned your back.

As if reading her mind, one of the women held a small child tighter by the shoulders, steering her toward the lodge, the one, and only familiar element on the horizon. Elle watched her movements, her grim stance. Maybe she thinks a great lizard will fly out of a cloud and carry the young ones away.

As days wore on, whoever didn't have the fishing fever would clamor for Key West, trying to figure out why anyone with a choice would settle here, why they would dredge, dig, burn and chop away the strangling vines and the lethal weeds, just to scrape what they could out of the soil. Even if there weren't so many on relief in Key West, Elle had made her peace with No Name Key and didn't suffer for lack of kin or company. She'd had her share of soup lines and living on the dole, going from one hovel to the next, always cold to the bone. Even when he managed to find work, Billy's temper would bubble up and they were sent on their way. The way she saw it, the road project was his last chance, and she was better off alone, though she knew he'd never see it that way and never let her stay in this place that she had grown to feel kindly towards. No, the fresh water and space of No Name Key sealed it for her. She would rather live with the rattlers, bugs the size of bats, the strange lizards in the underbrush. Found them comical, if truth be told.

4

"C'mon and walk back with us," he said, stopping the group's progress. But Elle shooed him away, nodding at the impatient crowd gathered in the sodden air. Monty tipped his cap to her. "Supplies," he said, patting a canvas-wrapped bundle inside a large wooden cart that also held the suitcases and trunks of the guests.

"I kin take it from here. Brought my own cart."

"No need."

"Don't want to take up space. Hard enough to get this in it." Elle thought of all the money it had cost to buy the new sink, saving it the way women always did — a few cents at a time and downplaying the cost — somewhere between handout and hardscrabble. Nothing Billy would tolerate if he knew, which he certainly did not.

"As you like," Monty said, setting the business part of the cart down by her feet. He raised his eyes to the tallness of her, a finger's width or so more than him. "You'll want to get this stashed by and by. Talk of a storm rising. First one this year. Some say the fewer there are, the more dangerous when they come."

Elle stared straight through him, mouth clenched against talking about what neither one of them could do anything about.

"What do I owe you?"

Monty hoisted the bundle into her cart, straightened up, and hushed her with his hand. "Nothin' to speak of. No worries, cuz, no worries. Billy don't know a thing."

"Here." Elle reached into her canvas pants and pulled out a packet with a couple of dollars in it. "Between the two of us. In your room, you'll find a couple of jars of stewed tomatoes by way of thanks. Those'll keep till spring."

"Don't suppose they'll get the chance."

She smiled. Men thought cooking and canning were her concessions to womanhood and were happy to find what they saw as a handle to her. She saw it as money, pure and simple.

"And make sure Sheila gets them settled with the sandwiches ready in the ice box. And tell her to get drinks first. Drinks are…"

"I know, Elle. Drinks more important than food. Sheila's a good girl. Knows the drill after the last few parties."

"I won't be gone but an hour. Before the train makes it in." Monty knew that Billy may have gotten a ride on the train and that she wanted to be ready for him.

Monty rearranged the cases, then turned, pulling the cart behind him, talking all the while, fast and loud. "Ladies first," he said, pointing to the lodge in sight, rising up green and golden. He moved serpentine through the pathways, like a great lizard, expertly avoiding the snarl of weeds and low tracts of brown-gray muck.

They didn't look back at her, their curiosity held by the peculiar surroundings. Once the group was finally out of sight, Elle lifted the canvas wrap and peeked inside. She nearly cried when she saw the shiny, white enamel sink, all proper-drilled with holes for the spout and the drain. *Next comes the stove,* Elle thought. *And more where that came from if I can just get to the orchard on time. Hermit always keeps to his word.*

Dog was pawing the ground, whimpering low, eager to be off. Elle gazed at the trail, smiling at the swishing skirts and city shoes, as the guests took their leave with trunks and trappings, the men curiously taking in the look of the land, not realizing that within a few days they would greet the landscape as if with a whip and a chair.

Once out of eyesight and earshot, Elle considered wheeling the cart to the lodge behind them and stashing the sink where Billy wouldn't find it. But since she hadn't expected so many guests on this first ferry, she decided to lay it up in thick brush by the pathway she took when running Dog. By afternoon, heavy heat would overtake the new arrivals. In no time they would be laying under fans, down for the count, and her time would be her own.

Dog barked, nosing her elbow. "Okay, okay." She needed to tend to the sapodillas. One tree she was excited about had an odd, saucer-shaped fruit, sweeter and juicier than any she had tasted.

But what she really wanted to do was run with Dog. He had started their runs, making her follow him till she looked forward to it, chasing after him, finding things she didn't expect in the woods. Only there she could shake off the dread and loneliness.

Elle jacked the cart a last few feet off into the brush, its bleached wooden sides perfectly camouflaged in the underbrush. She shuddered, imagining what would happen to her if Billy unearthed her plans. He was restless, bent on getting away from this place, but any kind of life with him seemed cursed by design. She carefully laid an armload of fallen palm fronds on the cart for insurance.

Freed of the company of people, she and dog ran past the secret pathways and the tangled branches, exhilarated by the newness of the woods. *If I can just have this small piece of time without him looking over my shoulder, without mouths to feed or plants to pick, I can face the rest.*

Maybe no one has ever traveled or seen this part, she thought as she ran, thrilled that not a single soul in the entire world knew exactly where she was. *Maybe I'm the only person who will ever set foot in this exact place.*

Dog owned this world, moving ahead of her, turning to see if she was behind him. He stopped and barked, wagging his tail so hard his body pivoted and he almost lost his balance. She stopped him from licking at a murky puddle, and soon her arms bore scratches and her cheeks looked like someone had slapped her. She took the red bandanna from her pocket and tied it around a branch to mark the spot. Then Dog was off, deeper into the woods, and Elle was surprised that it was so vast; she thought she knew it well. They must be dead center, having somehow lost the path to the sapodilla grove.

She called out, but Dog was gone—no bark, no sound. Elle stopped moving then looked around in the hot and windless woods, the foliage choking out the sun's rays. She expected to hear his clumsy, yellow body crashing through the trees. Any minute he would be upon her, toppling her over.

"Dog. Dog. Get on over here. Dog!"

A flat piece of coral big as a kitchen stool lay under a tall palm trunk, and Elle stopped and sat on it to catch her breath. Looking around, she thought she made out an echo in the forest.

After a bit, Elle wandered farther in, slipping between thick and battered palm trunks covered with bright red moss that hung like ragged, dirty lace. The place was maddening beautiful. Everything looked delicate but was huddled together, thick as old leather, protected against the brutal sun and salty air. Hopeful new growth peeked out from under the old, with leaves as bright as high polished emeralds.

Maybe Dog was chasing a lizard. *Doesn't eat them anymore, learned his lesson with the last one. Must've tasted real bad, even for Dog.* He could tolerate almost anything by the time she found him, living off insects and rodents for God knows how long.

One last try, then he'll have to find me at home. But she resisted abandoning him, fought the idea of one more loss, and moved deeper into the maze of scrubland.

Something held her tongue just as she was about to call out to Dog one more time. She turned, looking behind to where she thought the path might have been, and was relieved when she spied her red bandanna. Elle's gaze then returned to the flat stone, all the while gathering up her courage against what she couldn't conjure or see. Up ahead, a hazy ray of light broke through bushes and this lent her courage to call for Dog again, this time feverishly. The sound of her own desperate and broken voice surprised her and made her want to weep.

"Dawg. Dawwg. Where are you? Come here."

She heard a scratch and a muffled howl and suddenly he was in front of her, a small green apple in his mouth.

"Oh, Dog," she said as she scratched his face, pulled at his ears. "What do you have here?"

She reached and he moved his face away from her, thinking it was a game then dropped the fruit at her feet. "Where'd you get this from? Somebody got a grove of these?" Was it a kind of sun apple? Some sort of tropical fruit she'd never encountered before? She wanted to go back to find the spot, but it was getting late, and her time would be better spent checking that Sheila had gotten the guests settled or doing some picking. The train must be in, and she had to know if Billy had come. Maybe she would be lucky and he would stay away for the rest of the week and not hinder her work. Thinking about him caused her to dig red commas into her palms with her nails.

She dropped her hands and looked out through the thicket of greenery, pushing the dread of seeing Billy to the back of her mind.

Maybe the hermit's got a smaller grove he doesn't want me to find. Would be just like him. She smiled. *Let him have his secrets. Something we have in common.*

She thought of the old concrete cistern he let her have, the deed he gave her in exchange for tending his crops. But if he caught wind of her and Dog trespassing and didn't know who they were, she would've heard something by now—a gunshot most likely. She knew the rumors—the dead worker, him never charged with the killing.

One little peek is all. One little peek back, then I'll go home. Maybe I kin get me a branch and start one of my own.

She held the apple up to see it better. It was small—three inches around and very green. *Not yet ripe,* she thought, as she pushed her way back into the brush. Dog walked quietly by her feet. Not like him to be so wary, but it was no more than a little worrisome.

She saw the tree around the bend, apples spilled all about the ground.

What a joke. Only one spindly little tree. *No Name Key is never the lush Eden it appears to be. Always getting fooled by this place.*

She filled her pockets to bulging with the apples spilled on the ground and tossed one to Dog, who refused to run and fetch it.

"G'wan, go get it." She tossed another and he looked at her, his eyes runny. "Awright, something must've spooked you. Let's just get back before I catch it myself."

He ambled next to her, moving slowly, tail held low, all business, hunkering in close to her legs. *Could he have eaten a toad or some other creature he shouldn't have? Never mind. I'll get him some clean water.*

5

The walk back was much slower, took a good half hour. Elle pushed her mind past worries about Dog, instead moving it toward Billy, the guests and, finally, to the hermit's crops. First, she would get the cart with the sink stashed ten feet into an unmarked pathway. Dog moved slowly, tail down, and stopped at the edge of the wood, refusing to budge while she went in looking for the jumble of brown palm fronds that marked the cart's whereabouts. Dog began to retch as she cleared brush with her hands, getting good and scratched, bloodied by the secret thorns and invisible teeth on the stems of hardscrabble plants bent on survival.

Moving in toward the tangled seagrape and ragged leaves, Dog growled low and, then she heard a great thump. He began to whimper and whine then let out a low howl. She turned her body and was hit with a great, forceful blow to her midsection. She crashed backwards, some low-lying ferns cushioning her fall. Billy's tooled, leather face appeared like an apparition slicing through the vivid greenery. Dog was making noises somewhere between a whimper and a growl, afraid of what Billy would do to him if he advanced. Finally, he leapt forward, toppling Billy into the weeds with Elle. She moved to get up but Billy was over her, smacking her repeatedly across the face.

"Shut it," he said, although she hadn't uttered a sound. The lodge was within sight and someone might hear them. Elle thought it crazy how she conspired with him, her silence allowing him to get away with it again.

"Didn't expect me, huh? Came in on the train, stupid fool." His whisper ripped through her.

The train. They must have shooed him off the ferry. Then she composed herself, as she always did. He never stays long. Just a short while till he is back off to the work camp in Matecumbe. She just needed to hang tight a couple days.

"That what you been doing behind my back? Pilfering my money, making a home, when we already have one? That what you think you're about? Well, let me tell you something. I knowed it all along and let you get your pretty fixens' for the house. You think you're so smart, but remember that pretty woman just got off the ferry?" He saw the look on her face and carried on.

"Think back on it. The woman with the car? I'm talking at you." He screwed her head to face him. And she moved from her bed of sharp coral, ferns and ants, her back bent and head bowed, and before she could properly straighten up, he closed his hand and pounded the side of her head hard where it wouldn't leave a mark.

"My house you're building so pretty."

She didn't answer.

"Whose house?"

She shut her mouth hard, and he hit her again, until she thought better of keeping quiet.

"Whose fucking house is it?"

"Your house. It's your house, Billy."

"My house to sell to the pretty woman with the fancy dress."

She turned her head and saw a few people across the path, not quite within earshot—the pretty woman, and another with the boy. Would they think she and Billy were mating behind the bushes? She was mortified; more ashamed of having sex than she would be at submitting to his beatings. Either way it was an unwanted touch.

"Waiting for her husband to okay the deal. She won't do a thing without his say-so. Not like some I know."

He wrenched her arm to pull her up, and she fell on her knees again, but this time Dog was silent. She looked around, afraid he would propel her forward. But when she rose, Dog was hunkered over, heaving into the brush. She didn't want to fuss over him knowing how mad it made Billy when she paid mind to the animal. She swore he would be jealous of the sky if she said how beautiful it was. He pulled at her arm and pain shot through her shoulder.

"Might not go up to Matecumbe if we get a pretty penny for the house. Might just stay right here where I can keep an eye on you."

The woman eyed them as they made their way from the brush to the pathway, so Billy offered Elle his arm and made a small, tight smile as they passed her, nodding silent greetings. Dog limped behind them, barely able to keep up.

"What's wrong with him?" the woman asked. The boy broke from his mother and ran up to them. Dog's mouth was foaming, his eyes running, and he seemed about to topple over.

"Sick," the kid said, pointing. "Something wrong with

that dog." And Elle raced to Dog's side, knowing that Billy wouldn't lay a hand on either of them so long as witnesses were about. Dog tried to focus on her but was unable to move. He raised his paw, swayed and collapsed at her feet.

"Get me some water," she yelled, moving a strand of hair out of her eye, squinting at the kid. An apple rolled out of her pocket, half-eaten, pitted with teeth marks. Juice from the apple looked all right. She raised it to her nose, and it smelled faintly sweet, then like nothing at all. The kid ran off, and Billy gave her a look, but she didn't care.

Dog was fading fast, eyes lolling back in his head, tongue hanging out. She pulled him into a thicket of pigeon plums, laid his head to rest, and he began to wheeze from deep within. She ran across the spongy earth to the lodge and grabbed a bowl, ladling fresh water into it then raced back to the poor animal. His breathing was shallow, and she forced his mouth open, coaxed him to swallow, but he was too far gone. Feeling around his ribcage caused him pain, his heart vibrating in his chest.

By dusk, he had gone cold. Monty and Jim the fisherman pulled her off his stilled body and led her to her small room in the lodge, where she fell into a half sleep, staring at the dark blue posies on the half-finished wallpaper. She didn't blink when they passed the canvas tarp with the sink stashed by the outside wall near the lavatory. By sundown Dog had been mercifully laid to rest. Later that night, when all had returned to their cabins, and the lodge was quiet, she scrubbed the kitchen spotless, not stopping until her hands were raw.

6

Come morning, Billy seemed content and took her from behind, and she didn't protest—had to be quiet lest she wake the guest that would be stealing her house. He was in fine form, happy he had taken her measure. He told her he wouldn't return to Matecumbe until the woman's husband, Brushy, paid him off for Elle's little cement shack. "You know, Elle," he said, smacking her on the shoulder. "It won't be so bad. We'll have a bit of fun before we move back to Boston where things are bound to be better now that we have some means." But Elle's only surviving relative, Uncle George, would have nothing to do with her so long as she was with Billy. How many times had he told her so?

It would be no good for them there—breadlines were long, space was tight and jobs scarcer still. They left nothing, and they would return to the same; nothing but the shame of their neediness.

At No Name she had room and a shot at making it through, if she worked hard, saved some things, and made do without others. No Name Key was her last resort, the end of the road. Nowhere to run. Not south to Key West where only the rich get a stake and not north where you got bitter cold to add to your misery.

By afternoon, Billy was talking nonstop about getting out. "And don't think you can tell Brushy's missus what a torment it is to live here. I got my eye on you. No way she would listen anyhow, but I'm just sayin'. Don't need you to mess up my plans. Our plans."

He had the sink up in the room and Elle wondered if he had known all along what she was up to, watching the place get fixed up in secret. Getting more and more worked up till he came up with a trick to steal it from under her.

After Elle finished the afternoon cleanup, she stole away, planning to pick as many sapodillas as time would allow. Mosquitoes were staying away for some reason and even the birds didn't seem hungry. Something sat just outside her mind, and instead of going to the grove, she decided to retrace her steps from the previous day. It took a good twenty minutes to find the spot. When she finally arrived, she gasped when she thought it. The apples. It was the apples — the death apple tree — the manchineel.

Though they claimed they had felled them all, back before the lodge was built, they must've missed this one tree. She raced back in and spied the red bandana. Except for the fruit, it could have been any other tree, so unremarkable were the small, sharp green leaves, the grey trunk. The mangled look of the thing fit perfectly amongst the pigeon plums and mangroves.

A stash of freshly fallen apples lay at her feet and she picked one up and raised it to her nose. It smelled sweet, perfumed, and she was tempted to taste it but knew better. Dog had swallowed at least one of them, his mouth blistered and raw, his insides a match, no doubt.

Something told her to gather all the apples and keep her counsel about the tree's whereabouts. Maybe she would find a use for them sooner rather than later.

She could use the flesh to tempt rats trying to make nests in the walls. She could distill the juice, gain some know-how about the tree. It was bound to come in handy.

7

With an apron full of apples, she made her way back to the lodge to prepare for the fishing tournament festivities. No time to tend the hermit's groves; sapodillas and tomatoes would have to wait.

From the road, she heard activity coming from the lodge. Car engines regularly starting up, sending far off melodies crackling through the air. But the feeling of heaviness wouldn't leave the sky. Elle hurriedly worked through all she had to do, happy that she had two days to prepare for the party.

Fishing boats crowded the dock, arriving early for the tournament. Jim spotted her making her way to the lodge. "Need any help?"

He was always carrying things without being asked — a born gentleman. Bringing out ice blocks, hauling fish so she wouldn't have to bother with them. Whenever he had the time, he would filet fish and place them in the icebox without saying a word. His wife was a sweet faced, useless kind of woman whose coughing fits were the only thing she did well. They stayed in the cabin closest to the lodge, their narrow bed jammed against seasonal storage items and extra supplies for the lodge. He waited on her hand and foot, bending to fit his tall, skinny frame through the doorway, carrying treats from the lodge — board games, little sandwiches leftover from lunch. *He must be close to seven foot,* chuckled Elle to herself. More than once, he hit his head on a doorframe or low hanging lantern.

Jim's face was bright red from being on the water the day before. "I have a few hours off. If there's anything I can do to help?"

"Not necessary." *If Billy sees him around me, I'll really catch it.* "I got it all figured out. Party's day after tomorrow."

"No, ma'am. Just spoke to the owner, and he wants it a day early. All must be gone by Labor Day, he says. A storm seems to be brewing."

"He never said a word to me. You sure?"

Jim nodded yes.

"September is all. Worried about a storm for nothing. Fools," she said in a low voice.

When the ferry came in without Brushy, Billy glared at her as if she were to blame. That night, he gave her a look that had her make for the hummock hidden behind a stand of mangrove trees. Neither Monty searching for her in the dark, nor serpents or giant rats were enough to drive her back inside. At least poor Dog wouldn't catch it from Billy and, mercifully, the two of them had not managed to produce children to compound the misery. Thanks be for the knowledge of home cures — her stock of dried herbs and seeds, grown easily, just about anywhere. At first sign of discomfort, even before a missed monthly, her muddled concoction of pennyroyal and the bark of certain trees did what nature could not. Billy never understood what went wrong, although he was certain that she was the one who was cursed — as he liked to call it. Though he had no use for children, they were one more way to bind her to him. If he ever caught wind of her ministrations, he might kill her himself, that's for sure.

Next morning, on the way back to the lodge from gathering eggs, Elle made the rounds of the cabins and spied Mrs. Rowlands, the good looking woman, lying out on her screened-in veranda, crunching on ice chips supplied by her maid, her butterfly sleeves stock-still in hushed air. The woman and her maid eyed her, and Elle felt constantly watched, like something was about to pounce.

She didn't dare go to her small cement house, hoping the whole matter would blow over. Billy was just trying to get a rise out of her. The more she thought on it, the more certain she was that he was just being mean. What would a woman like that want with a little shack in these parts? She sure don't do no fishin'.

When they weren't out fishing, guests mostly stayed in their small cabins dotted alongside the lodge, going to the main building for card games, books, or meals, although they had stoves and water and could cook if the spirit moved them.

Elle heard the tap-tap of heels, muted on the hall's thick linoleum floor. She pushed up her sleeves and wondered who was outside her kitchen.

Mrs. Rowlands called out to her. "Mrs. Woodman. I've come to have words with you." Elle poked her head out the swinging door to the hallway. Mrs. Rowlands was wearing a dress so white Elle almost had to avert her eyes.

Elle wiped her hands on her apron then ran one through her hair, getting egg on it. Mrs. Rowlands looked at her, not bothering to disguise her contempt. "Billy, I mean Mr. Woodman, says that the place should be ready by next month, October at the latest. He tells me the sink has arrived and a small stove is on its way."

Stove? What a line. But something about this lie told her that Billy was serious about selling the place.

"I'm talking to you. I said we expect you to have it ready by October."

Ha, October. Guess she don't know much about how time works out here.

"Don't know nothin' about no stove. Suppose it's him what'll be getting it."

"Don't play coy with me. He warned me about you." Squinting into the light, she had the look of a slattern about her, despite her fine clothes.

A door slammed at the back of the lodge and someone came, heavy-footed, to the kitchen.

"You oughta not be talkin'," Billy said, cutting into their conversation. He shrugged his shoulders and pointed at Elle. "She don't know nothing about it. She's just done a small part. The right hand don't never know what the left is up to."

Billy wore khaki workpants tucked into boots and a shirt with the sleeves cut off. He was all sinew and cabled muscle, dark from working in the sun. Elle saw the way Billy looked at Mrs. Rowlands and she back at him, and Elle felt something akin to pity for the woman. Here she was, all the money and choice in the world, and she bothers with him?

Billy stared hard at the woman, willing her to walk out of the room, then followed, hot on her trail. Elle heard the whispering, Billy's voice rising, "I told you to wait."

The tone was familiar to Elle, words knocking into one another, till he was good and worked up. But Billy surprised her when he righted his voice and she understood something that she had never before figured out. He could control his fists when he had reason. He just liked using them, pure and simple. The woman moved on down the hallway, the screen door whined open and then closed. Silence. Then Billy pushed the swinging kitchen door so hard it slammed against the counter.

"I got no time for this," Elle said. "Labor Day party needs preparing."

"Won't have to do that for much longer."

Elle looked past him to the long fish knife with the flat, narrow blade. "I don't know how much you think that shack's worth. Not enough to keep a dog in fleas."

"You know it and I know it, but she don't know it. Leastways, don't care." Billy winked at her, then wandered over to the window and pulled the curtain back. And Elle understood that the woman was gone because Billy said to her, "And don't never think you can get away because it ain't gonna happen."

She reached for the grunts, laid them on the butcher block, cut off their heads, and began rolling them in egg, then the flour mixture. "Owners are coming and we got near to a full house."

"Won't be waiting on them much longer. Just on me, like you should."

"Got to get the limes from out back of the well when I finish here." But he made no sign of leaving. "Owners comin' any time now," she said.

"Go figger," he said, looking at her, his eyes flat and narrow. Any minute he could go from a dead stop into a hot storm rising. Elle rested the knife on the small butcher block and pursed her lips into a sad little smile as he reached for her.

"You know how much you love the feel of me," he said. "Put the latch on."

When Elle motioned to go to her room, he nodded "no", pulled her toward the pantry, and ripped at her apron, pulling her skirt up. Elle glanced out the window and saw the woman looking up into the shuttered window, waiting. She closed her eyes tight and willed him to finish. Quick.

Finally, he let her alone, and she tried to find a tempo, moving to hide her shaking, more from fear of someone walking in on them, than of him. His uncommon nose always caught the scent of what she was up to. This time it told him that she liked it on No Name Key and didn't have the heart to follow him any longer. So she had to go along, convince him that she would do whatever he wanted. After washing and drying her hands, she changed her apron, finished breading the grunts, and placed breakfast loaves into the oven to bake. She picked up his shirt from the floor, watching him head off, showing off his fool anchor tattoo that spread across his chest.

Then she headed outside behind the lavatory to set up a table for butchering one of the prize swordfish before bringing it in to complete the finer dressing.

Monty found her there. He was carrying a megaphone and a long streamer of paper lanterns. "Got a fine looking warbler coming in on the train. Gonna go pick her up, and the band as well. Everything all right?"

"Oh, sure."

"Sorry about the sink. Thought Billy would be gone by now."

"Me, too," Elle said. "No one's fault, and he says he'll be gone day after tomorrow. Same time as most of the partygoers."

"Many talking about leaving early. Seems a storm is brewing. Might be a big one."

"Seems to me there's always someone claiming secret knowledge," Elle said, not looking up from her work. "When the sapodillies are plenty, when the animals don't eat, when the sky goes green."

"Or purple," he said, smiling.

She raised her eyes to his. It was nice to talk of nothing at all. Bad enough to face the evil that is than to go about pining for more.

She shooed him away, and Monty tipped an imaginary hat at her then ambled off, paper lanterns dragging behind him.

The prize swordfish, longer than she was tall, lay in a cart filled with ice. She wheeled it out back of the lodge and eyed the butcher-block sawhorse. The fish was so big that she placed the top plank on the ground to lay the fish out for butchering. She donned the rubber apron and boots then reached for a heavy cleaver lying nose down in a pail. She chopped the spear off with precision and held it closer to inspect. It looked like a long, sharp tooth coming to a razor thin point. The fish stared up at her and she swiftly dealt the neck a series of whacks with the cleaver, then used the hacksaw, working steadily, finally finishing the job by slamming through bone with the cleaver until it was narrow enough to twist off. She flung the severed head into a large washbasin with a thud.

8

Wind carried the murmurs of Billy and the Rowlands woman, but they weren't close enough for Elle to make out words. After Labor Day, Elle would ask the hermit if Billy really had gotten ahold of the house deed. More likely, he was a liar, but she had to know for sure. In the meantime, she must stay calm, prepare breakfast and box lunches for thirty, start supper, and do what she could to keep Billy quiet and get him on that ferry before the owners decided she wasn't worth the trouble.

"Hey, Elle. That's where you are. Families hungry." It was Sheila, the second cook, brought in for the party.

"Guess all that good fishing sharpened their appetites. Sorry, but I got to get this done before it spoils." The zinc icebox couldn't hold large fish, so they had to be butchered as soon as they arrived, which was her job when no one else claimed it.

"Owners want to have words when you're done here."

She carried on cutting it down to size and tossing the bones into the pail. Pin bones pulled out easily then she slid the knife under the gill, dipping in above the long, flat spine, slicing through flesh in a long, clean run. Dog loved to watch her work and swordfish was his favorite. Seemed he could smell it from wherever he was and come running.

All day long she rushed the preparations, trying to shake feelings of impending doom. Everything around her felt dull and heavy, as if she were being tilted, pressed into darkness, despair and cold. *What did the owners want to tell her?* How many would love this place she had carved for herself? A cook always ate. She needed to do up this feast to make up for the trouble Billy was bound to cause. He was bad for business, and she saw the looks and heard the whispers. They were being watched.

9

Worry accompanied her to the grove, where she filled a wooden bowl with fresh key limes, a perfect shade of yellow. Then to the pantry to make the broiled grapefruit and potted, smoked fish, a treat for the men's lunches on their last fishing trip. She would try out her recipe for sapodilla pie, lay in a good store of key lime pies, some grits and grunts, and spoonbread. Maybe do up some Latin favors, but mostly good and hearty American fare. She liked the feel of the food, the smells. Instruments slicing through flesh and steam rising from pots on the stove gave her a satisfaction she could lose herself in. Whenever she opened the door to the pantry to find potted smoked fish and dried goods, she stood back and took it in. No matter how often, she never tired of seeing so much food in one place.

Let him sell the wretched shack so long as I can stay in this place. But she knew he had begun to sniff out her desire to stay, and it set familiar fears upon her. Whenever she gained comfort and contentment, Billy demanded they leave. *Time to move on,* he would say. *Nothing more for us here.*

But nothing had got under her skin like this strange little island where people were few and she could finally keep her own counsel.

After assembling thirty cold lunch kits for the early fishing expedition and placing them in the icebox, Elle prepared the egg and vegetable aspic, pouring gelatin slow and evenly before leaving it to set overnight. Night was upon her by the time she was done so she cleaned by lamplight, something she disliked because the job was never as thorough as she liked. She was so exhausted that she wanted to crawl into bed with her apron on. After a bit, she heard Billy's soft footfalls. He opened the door carefully, and stood in silhouette against moon glow from the window, not bothering to come to her side and make sure she was asleep. He closed the door gently behind him and she was grateful to hear the soft sweep of his footsteps move down the ramp.

Sometime late into the night, she awoke and he was still missing. She had dreamt about her unfinished house carried out to sea on huge waves, Dog barking in the window, unable to escape. Had he really gotten the deed from the hermit? She knew he had left his buckram sack somewhere in the tool room, never bringing it inside her room. She would be able to hear him return, she thought, so she pulled on her housedress and made for the back of the lodge.

She found his drawstring buckram sack stuffed with a brown envelope of old photos of her family, photos that she thought had been lost long ago. She took the envelope out and tiptoed back, barefoot, careful, although she was alone in the lodge. Those long-ago photos were taken before her parents died. Her uncle George had taken shots of the three of them smiling, clowning around under their tall tree in Boston at Christmastime.

And Elle knew in an instant that Billy was so jealous that he would deny her the comfort even of her own blood. She pushed back her anger and sorted through the rest of the photos before tucking them all into her mattress.

Billy and the woman were gone well into the wee hours, on an adventure, finally coming in just before dawn. The cabin next to the woman's was full, and the chance they were taking must've added spice to the thing. Oh, yes, that Rowlands woman looked the part if you knew what you were looking for. Elle felt the whole of her tiny paradise slipping away. Next thing she knew, she wouldn't even be fit for the whorehouse in Key West that Billy forever threatened her with. Elle pulled the threadbare sheet off her damp body, a fly buzzed back of her neck.

10

The owners had arrived the day before to take guests on the traditional pre-Labor Day fishing junket, and Elle awoke troubled, concerned she had fallen behind on her chores. She rose early, fed the chickens corralled behind the large boulder to keep them from disturbing the guests.

On her way out, she saw the Rowlands woman watching her from the clearing. *What had Billy said to her? What were they planning?* But what did it matter anyhow? So long as she had a place here, she could ride out whatever they cast in her path. Elle was almost embarrassed by how much beauty she saw in this weird place and how much she dreaded leaving it, ill-wind, or no. It was more than a home to her. It had the feel of providence.

Fewer guests than usual were joining this Labor Day celebration. Talk of the storm drove many away early, but nothing could discourage the hard-core fishermen amongst them. Elle headed back to the lodge with a basket of eggs, her mind full—the thought of losing Dog, Billy and the woman with burning eyes laughing at her troubles, Billy keeping her photographs. It was just too much to contend with right now. He couldn't help letting her know what she was in for, couldn't resist gloating.

Once she was across the clearing, Billy was on her. "Mrs. Rowlands's husband coming in today for sure, so don't count on me leaving here anytime soon. Best I wait here and unload that thing some might call a hovel." His eyes narrowed, seeing nothing but her. The thought that someone might be around emboldened Elle and she spoke back.

"Not yours to sell," Elle said, and before Billy could react, she moved quickly, dodging him, then skipped over a puddle, hoping to see vacationers, but none were up yet.

"Just wait till tonight," he whispered.

The water had begun to lap strangely towards shore, as if it had a heavy undertow. The sky was flat and green, and no birds sang. It was eerie, dulled-down, and silent. Elle wiped sweat trickling down the back of her neck. The underside of her hair was wet and curled.

She spent all day making the side dishes and a store of sapodilla pies. She remembered hearing of a time when key limes lay spoiling on the ground. No one had known how to handle them, until someone had the wit to make a key lime pie. As she mashed the sapodilla and mixed it with eggs and cream, she imagined workers carting the huge sapodilla fruit away after the harvest, money changing hands, all while she took a snooze on a shaded hammock. In just a few short years, the sapodilla would be as common as the Florida orange. She was sure of it. She rolled the dough, lining up the pie plates — six key lime and six sapodilla cream pies. Tonight her recipe would get its first big audition.

Happily, the owners' niece, Sheila, helped her as second cook, doing the peeling and washing up. But Elle could not quite lose herself in the contentment of the kitchen, even as she lay out a feast, anticipating the oohs and aahs of guests impressed with her handiwork. Old man Rowlands had not shown up, so Billy would be in a right mood tonight.

By dinnertime, Billy was doing everything not to look at the Rowlands woman, on his best behavior, not even sneaking drinks. He had even tackled a few odd jobs to ingratiate himself, and Elle was beginning to wonder if she might get through his visit unscathed after all. The band was playing a light melody of gentle dinnertime tunes on stage, chatter coming in waves. Elle went out back to bring in ice to be chopped for drinks. It melted as quickly as she could haul it in, so she hacked off a larger piece and wrapped it in a towel, tired of the trips back and forth. She heard something in the sky closing in on No Name. A plane hovered overhead and dropped something so close to the lodge that Elle heard it hit the ground. She raced to the center of the field and picked up a bright red bag weighted with rocks. Inside was a notice warning all to evacuate the next day. She hid it in the larder, waiting for the right moment to talk to the owner.

The party was picking up by now. Trophies were being awarded, saving first prize for last. In between dabbing at sweat forming around the upper lip and temples, women were fanning shiny faces, trying to keep their hair from flattening or frizzing in the dank heat. Streaks of black eyebrow paste ran down the sides of a young blonde's nose, making her look like a demented bird. Giant mechanical fans moved slowly, pushing around the fetid air, the whiny noise barely earning the small comfort they brought.

Monty steered Billy back to the table by the kitchen. Elle made out bits of the conversation.

"You gotta go back soon, Billy. You won't have the work if you wait too long." But Billy's mouth was set in a horizontal line, teeth showing when he tried to smile.

Monty sent a tray of drinks to the band and smiled like a banshee when the fine looking songstress downed hers. She looked at Monty and sang.

No one to talk with
All by myself
No one to walk with
But I'm happy on the shelf
Ain't misbehaving
I'm savin' my love for you

Monty toasted the stage and Elle moved up behind him, saying, "Watch your back, Mr. Monty. She sure looks like trouble to me."

Elle spotted the owner and showed him the notice. He said he would be taking off right after dessert, and would she see to it that everyone got on the morning ferry, no exceptions. And make sure Billy and Monty locked the place up good, put the shutters on tight before the storm. "No need to mention anything before dinner. Let's all stay calm, not spook the crowd, or spoil the party."

After the main course, the wine and beer flowing, the owner took the stage. "Seems a storm is brewing and we got to take caution, no matter how many false warnings we get in these parts. Tomorrow, sending an extra ferry to pick everyone up and take you all, in comfort, back to the mainland."

This announcement had the effect of everyone simultaneously calling for a round of drinks. Most smiled stupidly, happy to share in the great adventure. While they were getting more drinks, he continued, "This little gal here, my niece Sheila, has made you all a little surprise. We're calling it Bananas Sheila, an old-fashioned banana custard ringed with ladyfingers. New specialty of No Name Key Lodge."

Elle had her sapodilla pie at the ready but realized that in all the worry, she had forgotten to tell the owner to announce it. She supposed she could quietly serve it to the guests and wait for the compliments to come rolling in. Her famous key lime pies were also lined up on the table, but everyone asked for Sheila's new creation.

"When did you make these?" Elle asked, distressed that the only takers for her pies were the youngsters who would soon be put to bed.

"You were gone, and I wanted to give them something different, something special to celebrate. You been preoccupied."

It was true. She had rushed through the preparations, couldn't concentrate with fruit about to spoil and Billy threatening her at every turn.

The music was languid, everyone was calm, and the room was humming. The Rowlands lady, red lipstick and all, was smiling like a fool, and the owner looked from her to Billy as if he were beginning to suspect something. When he saw Elle watching him, he looked away.

Billy was trouble; the owners want him out. *And me with him.*

Elle tended the tables, tidying, picking things up, and while carrying a load that was too heavy, she brushed against the side of a chair and sent a pitcher of water crashing, ice cubes careening across the floor.

"Here, let me help." Sheila bent over to collect them, whispering, "You need some rest. You need to calm down.

You're nervous as a cat."

"Who says? Your uncle?"

"Don't need anyone to tell me. Plain as the nose on your face."

As Elle tidied tables to make room for dessert, Sheila made her way into the kitchen, returning with a large tray of individual banana custards fenced in by ladyfingers. Joe emerged from the back with a bottle and then, in an unbroken movement, drizzled a steady stream of Pirates Rum over them. He finished by flicking a lighter and flambéing the lot of them with a obvious pride.

"Bananas Sheila — new specialty of No Name Key Lodge. Tell your friends. Can't get it nowhere else," Joe said.

The room clapped, someone whistled, others oohed and aahed as they were served. Sheila watched sympathetically as Elle cleared up the last of the cutlery.

Billy was completely oblivious to her defeat — standing in front of her key lime and sapodilla pies, barely touched, with Sheila where Elle should be, center of the crowd, accepting accolades — while she acted the common drudge, picking up the slops.

The Rowlands woman came up to her from behind and whispered in her ear, "The fish was dry."

II

From the corner of her eye, she caught the Rowlands woman and Billy exchange glances. Elle put a warm hand to Billy's shoulder. "Just hold on, I got something for you when they all done," she nodded at the band, "something just for us."

"Bout time you did something for me." Billy probably imagined that she was jealous of the other woman so she took her leave, asking Sheila to please begin the washing up.

An island tune was playing while Sheila handed out more complimentary paper fans that unfurled to reveal a printed image of No Name Key Lodge, a map of the Florida Keys with a big dot marking the lodge, along with the mailing address.

Patrons began to dance languidly, but Elle was sweating cold, making her shiver in the hot room. She could not push Billy away any longer. He had squeezed his way into her mind, kicking inside her skull with steel-toed boots, each strike sharp and pounding.

Mrs. Rowlands eyed her as Elle slipped out the door, holding a giant, empty pickle jar by the neck. On the side of the building, she crouched at the root cellar, feeling around for the basket of apples collected after Dog died. With the party in full swing, no one would notice her absence, so she took the fish filet knife and peeled and chopped a half dozen apples into a fine pulpy mess, careful to extract the sweet smelling nectar into the mouth of the jar before discarding the debris. She was careful to wash any fruit juice off her hands before pumping water into the jar. She shook the concoction vigorously, and it mixed up to form a good half-quart that she stashed back in the root cellar.

Drinks continued to flow, music blasted out, the tempo increasing. The party was on the upswing, men reciting details of the fish that got away or stories about one they caught the year before. A conga line formed. In the kitchen, Elle stacked dishes, and Sheila began the washing up, unable to completely hide the look of triumph at her culinary achievement.

"Billy says he's leaving on the morning ferry," Elle lied, hoping Sheila would relay this information to the owner.

"Won't be a soul left here, from what I can tell. You going too?" Sheila asked.

"Oh, sure," Elle lied again. "Better to get now. No telling how long the weather will keep. Really blowing now; don't know if there'll be a second ferry. Not reliable at the best of times."

When Elle wandered to the party, she heard the owner ask Billy to start nailing the shutters on the side of the lodge furthest away from the guests. Soon Elle heard the steady bang-bang of shutters and screws as he attached the heavy metal sheets to the doors and windows of the lodge.

By the time Elle made it to her room, Billy was tired of being on good behavior.

"Always watching me. Glad your boss blowed on outta here. Which is what some say I should do." He couldn't resist adding, "even if others would rather I stay." He waited then for her to give him any kind of a sign that she cared, so she smiled and went up to him.

"Got summit for the two of us. Cadged it from the party. Wait here."

He sat on the narrow bed, eyebrows knit together. "Where you up to?"

"Surprise. You'll see. Like the old days."

He leaned over and began undoing his bootlaces. Elle headed outside, behind the lavatory, to the fish-butchering place, and reached into the root cellar for the pickle jar with the bone-colored juice. Back in the kitchen lodge, she grabbed a bottle of high-proof white rum she used for cooking, some simple syrup, and made a cocktail of it, putting the lid on the jar and shaking it until it got frothy. Before tiptoeing to the room, she removed her apron, smoothed her hair, and pinched her cheeks. On her way past the mirror in the hall, she bit her lips to make them red.

She stood in shadow, in the doorway, framed in light from the open window. He was sitting on the bed, in darkness, save for a shaft of light that traced the fine bulge of his shoulder muscle. She tried to recall the thrill of seeing him unclothed and adjusted her tone.

"You been working hard," she said, her voice low.

"Thought you'd never notice."

"I notice much mor'n you suppose. Like the woman for example."

"She don't mean a thing to me. Just a way to get outa here. Only you an' me. What you got there?"

"Here," she said. "Like I said, you been working hard.

Workin' for us." She swallowed when she said it, choked the words out.

Elle stood over Billy as he sat on the corner of the bed, then moved the kerosene lamp to the center of the painted bureau and struck a match on the sole of her shoe. She lit the wick and replaced the glass shade.

"Tired," he said, and she knew having sex had to be his idea. It had been so long that she forgot how this played out. So long that she had forgotten what it was like to want him. She remembered it with a sickening lurch.

"Here, have this," she said, her eyes bright.

"What's gotten into you? You never liked me drinking."

He looked lost, and the old pity rose up in her, and she hesitated then placed the jar away from him, on the floor.

"Let's just get us some sleep," she said. "Another long one tomorrow. You got to get out of here, got to get back up to camp or there'll be nothin' left for you. They'll give your job away. Lots waiting in line for it, and for my job, too."

"Not going back."

"Never?"

"Never. And you're goin' with me. Got the money from the woman. Not even waiting on her husband; she got some of her own. That's what we were doing yesterday."

"What would she want with a run-down hovel like that?" Elle asked. "Not even on lodge property, almost in the woods."

"Getting it for her servant lady. And maybe she wants to do me a good turn. It don't make no difference to her. She got cash, and lots of it." His voice had begun to level, getting the empty tone that told her to stop quizzing him.

"So what you want to do if you ain't going back? Can't stay here."

"Don't plan to."

Elle decided it was best to quit talking.

"Leaving soon as her old man comes, even if he don't. I told you she already paid me something for that shack of yours." He smiled slyly. "Then we'll be off on the ferry, along with the best of them. Might even pay the fare this one time. Show those bastards."

Elle nodded, worn out from all the banter. Fatigue from her long hours of toil set in and, she was beyond caring when he turned her shoulder, pulling her toward him.

"You tryin' to do something nice for me? I don't care a fig for that strumpet in a fancy dress. Always you, Elle. You'n me. If only you knowed it."

Elle nodded, stiffening. The notion of them coupling again, him with his unnatural appetites, was too much to bear.

"Here. Been a long day." She reached for the jar.

"Why you bringin' me drink?"

"You're right. Just wanted us to have our own celebration, but it were a stupid notion." Elle stood up and reached for her flowered housedress flung across the bed. "I'll dump this stuff before anyone gets wind."

"Whoa. Pass it over."

The screened window by the bed was open, the air sticky with heat. A curl of flypaper loosed from the ceiling and landed on the bed, making her jump.

"Skittish as a schoolgirl. Though sure don't look like one." He didn't bother to flick the flypaper away. Elle got up and closed the window, drawing the pleated paper blind.

"Hey, hot enough in here. Suppose you don't want no one to hear. Always was a shy one."

He was warming to the hunt, not so interested in the

drink now that he thought she wanted him to have it.

"Glad you're not drinking. Not good for you. Gets you too riled up. Don't know what I was thinking on." Again, Elle reached for the pickle jar, the thick, almost congealed contents warm to her touch. "Not looking too appetizing, best to toss it out."

"Nothin' touched by your hands is ever less than divine," he said, moving her hand to his crotch.

She pulled away and grabbed the pickle jar with both hands.

"Hey. Gimme that," he said.

"Hold yer horses," she said and shook the jar, back and forth over her shoulder as if it were a giant cocktail shaker. In the dim light of the kerosene lamp, she made out a half inch of foam. "Can't vouch for the taste but it's bound to pack a punch. But still, maybe you shouldn't..."

He moved the tangle of sheets away from his midsection and pulled the jar from her. It was an awkward size, and the slow moving liquid swished back and forth like an evil tide.

Elle watched in fascination as Billy held it over his shoulder like a plug of moonshine, took a chug, then spit it out with such force that it slammed into the wall.

"What the hell you got in there?"

"White rum maybe mixed with something more fierce." He was staring at her, his face intense and puzzled. She reached for it again, shaking her head, murmuring, "Sorry, a mistake."

But before she could rise from the sweat soaked sheets, he grabbed the jar from her and held it away, treating it as a game. "Last time I drank something like this, I woke up four hours later, half-naked in the middle of the street five miles from the house." He winked at her, raising the liquid to his lips as she held her breath. In great loud gulps, he chugged the entire jar.

"Yohoo! Sure is hot stuff. Tastes like Apple Jack, only sweeter."

She was sitting on the bed inching away from him. His face began to show a slight puffiness. It happened so quickly she thought she must be imagining it. He looked ruddy, even in such dull light.

"Water. Get water."

"On my way," she said, keen to exit the tainted room.

She grabbed her housedress, slid out the door, one arm struggling to find the sleeve, and made her way to the kitchen, listening, nerves pinging, straining to hear any sound, looking for light. She forced her arm through the sleeve, catching a finger on the seam, ripping the cheap, worn fabric. She didn't see any lights out the kitchen window, only the silhouettes of three cabins — one belonging to Mrs. Rowlands.

She heard him move first, followed by a thud against the door. When the door moaned, she raced over and slammed it shut from the outside.

"E-l-l-e. Help me."

He began kicking at the door to open it, and Elle panicked, terrified the noise would wake someone. But the lodge was silent, Monty last seen weaving drunkenly down the pathway, heading for the farthest cabin, the singer in tow.

She reached for an ironstone pitcher on the counter, pushed her way into the small room, and found him on the floor, one hand around his throat, the other reaching in, fingers trying to pry his airway open. His lips were blistered, his face like a puffer. Instead of grabbing onto the pitcher she offered, he tackled her legs and she went down, landing on his chest. He let out a great groan and she placed her knee against his neck and pushed it in hard, trying to crush his throat. He flailed, pinned and helpless under her muscled knee, and she stared down at him with a surge of hatred.

The pitcher hurtled across the floor, banging against the skirt of the bureau. Elle turned for a brief second, loosening her knee from against his throat. The pickle jar was still upright when she reached for it with both hands and brought it down on his head with such force the glass broke around his face, blood starting to spurt from his head. He braced himself, cutting his hands in the glass shards on the floor and inched sideways like a demented crab. She leaned over him and he grabbed a fistful of her hair, yanking her head toward him, but the effort was too much for him. He began to retch and moved a hand away to grab hold of his throat, his breathing now a rasping whistle. Elle moved up and away from him, and he swung his feet at the spindly table holding the kerosene lamp. He's trying to tip it over, set the place on fire. She moved quickly to right it, but it crashed to the floor. She barely managed to grab the lamp and blow out the flame in time.

The room was completely dark. She heard him trying to catch his breath. Blood pulsed terrible waves of fear through her. Billy's breathing became shallow, more urgent, as he tried to push out air through his nose, as if he were trying to call her name.

Quickly, Elle darted to the window, opening the shade to peek outside. She heard noise behind her before Billy tackled her, slicing at her thigh with a large piece of glass, opening it up, causing blood to gush from a jagged wound. Elle fell to her knees but instead of pain, she felt a great tide of rage that so blinded her in white light she didn't realize she was smashing his head with the metal pitcher until the fourth or fifth strike. Finally, he groaned, and she let go of the pitcher and grabbed for her yellow blouse, tying it tightly around her leg, the blood quickly staining the cloth.

Elle willed away the pain, too stunned to feel anything but thickly spreading panic. He was on the floor, making gurgling sounds, and she picked up the pitcher one last time and slammed it into his head with such force that he released his last breath in an exhaled rattle. Elle fell backward, her arms poker-hot and stinging.

Silence filled the room, and the bloody smell of iron and shit hung in the dank air like an overpowering curtain. She hobbled, half-slid to the window. Moonlight flushed the tiny room with light, turning the blue posies on the wallpaper to a sickly green, like a scene from the wax museum. Her thigh had a jagged gash six-inches long, and she pressed into it and tied the blouse tighter around it, distributing the pressure as evenly as she could. It throbbed like a captive animal, but still she felt no pain.

When she dared turn to Billy, he looked like something strange coughed up by the sea, already bloated, decayed. It was done. In a drawer she found a small pair of snips and cut a piece of sheet from the bottom, ripping it to make a bandage that she tied around her leg.

She righted the lamp, carefully searching for spilt kerosene, but not finding any, she lit it. Her mind moved rapidly through broken images — faces, pathways, ways of escape, ferry schedules, breakfast for the guests, Dog — and she kicked at his body, hard, to see if he would move. Still afraid to get too close, she heard no sound, sensed no movement.

He could be faking it. He was wily, always full of surprises.

She stared for a full minute, fixing her eyes on his chest, his ruined face, closely searching for any sign of life. The room was smeared in blood, knotted sheets soaked in it lay on the floor. Broken glass and handfuls of hair glued in place by congealing pools of blood.

No one ever comes in here. Still.

Elle opened the door to the hallway, glancing nervously back at Billy, then closed it, changed the bandage with another strip of torn sheet, and pulled on her canvas pants. Finally she exited the room, half-limping down the ramp and out to the pump behind the lavatory. She found the cart that she used to haul the big fish to be butchered. She pulled at the folded tarp sitting by the pump, placed it on the cart, and wheeled it up the ramp and down the narrow hallway to her room, her leg almost giving way, sharp pain suddenly shearing her flesh, coming in swells.

12

Even if she tipped the cart at an angle, it was still too big to get through her bedroom doorway. She listened for sounds but found only silence. How long until first light? Was the sky beginning to pink? No, it was still a thick black.

When Elle opened the door to her bedroom, she half-expected Billy to be sitting up, or gone, maybe crouched behind the door, ready to jump at her, maybe hiding in the closet. But he was as she had left him, stiffening by the minute. She dragged him out by his heels, her thigh beating like a demented heartbeat as she held the cart sideways and rolled him into it, wedging his head over his chest. With all her strength, she moved to the side and righted the cart, Billy settling into the center in a half-seated slump. She tented him with a tarp, her senses sharp, watching and listening, terrified at being spotted. On the way down the hall, Elle caught a glimpse of her expression in the mirror and a shock of terror coursed through her. Her blood-smeared face looked the very image of murder. But she was in it now, so she steered the cart quick and true down the ramp, onto the walkway and turned sharply to the back of the lodge.

Now what? Could she roll him under the crouch space under the shack? A pail of water, still warm from the unrelenting heat, reflected light from the moon. She immersed her hands in it then splashed some on her face as best she could, finally pouring it over her head, trying to soften some of the quickly drying blood lest someone come upon her. Something moved and she jumped, but it quickly scurried away—a small orange cat. Elle moved the cart deeper in the shadows around the side of the house. Still, no lights flickered in the cabin windows. *Thank God for the Labor Day piss up. Everyone sleeping it off.*

I have no choice, she thought when she spied the long, wide plank on the sawhorse. She pulled it off, placed it on the ground and dumped Billy on to it. The long cleaver was ready in the pail where she had left it. Kneeling above his body, she thought she saw an eyelid flutter just before she slammed the thick blade down across his throat. Ten times more to guillotine his head. She tossed his head into the pail and methodically dismembered the rest of his body. She imagined him as an ungainly animal, focusing first on the large joints, one after another, shutting her mind to the true nature of the task.

Just before finishing, the blade slipped and sliced through the flesh under her fingers, cutting a horizontal slash through her hand. She held back from crying out and bandaged her wound with a strip of the bedclothes. Exhausted, she did not have the strength to tackle his torso. She rolled it onto the ground and placed the plank over it, making out a loud buzzing as the flies, now assembling in clouds, became more aggressive.

The air was thick, heavy, and motionless, and the telltale stench of rust hovered around her, getting into her clothes, under her fingernails, coating the hair in her nostrils. A large, maddened insect dove at her head. She crushed it with her hand and it crawled across her temple. Elle had to dig it out of her ear, almost making her lose her balance.

Large crab traps, piled against the icehouse, formed towers, and Elle pulled a short stack of them toward her, placing bits of him in easily, grateful for their size. The large traps were almost three feet across, with narrow openings, making it difficult to force his limbs through. Once filled, she moved them behind the empty ones, covering them with tarps. Her shoulders burned with the effort. Moving quickly, Elle made her way back to the kitchen pantry and grabbed a pair of waxed tablecloths then went to the back room for Billy's duffel and gunnysack. She emptied out the contents on her bed and closed the door behind her.

A great horde of insects hovered over the traps, buzzing loudly, jostling to get under the tarps, battling amongst themselves to get at him. Noise filled her ears and bites soon stung her flesh as she wrapped his hacked torso in the bed sheet. She was finally able to wedge it into the gunnysack, ripping a seam to get it properly covered. The last thing she saw was his crude anchor tattoo as it disappeared into the coarse fabric. Gratefully, his head fit easily into the duffel.

Still dark, she rinsed out the cart, upended it against the pump, filled a pail with water, and poured it over herself.

In the darkness, she washed herself, over, and over, letting the stream of blood sink into the parched earth until the crusted blood on her scalp softened and dissolved and she no longer felt the stickiness. The air was so thick and hot that sweat seeped into her wet shirt, affording her no chance to truly dry off. Elle finally limped back up the ramp, a pail of water swinging in one hand, a rag in the other. Backtracking from her room, she scrubbed at the bloody cart tracks in the hallway.

Once inside, under lamplight, the room revealed its horrors. Elle gathered the sheets and clothing, and placed glass shards in the center of the pile, bundling them up and moving the mess into the metal trashcan for burning. She spent the wee hours scrubbing floors and walls, her hand and leg throbbing and swollen, her mind empty and numb. After rinsing out her soiled clothing, she raided the linen closet for another sheet and blanket, but then thought better of it. The remaining linen was too fancy and might bring attention to her.

At first light, Elle walked back to the traps, the furor of rushing insects forcing her to move faster. Her hands safely inside a pair of men's work gloves, she righted the cart and placed crab pots in it, carefully covering them with the tarp. Wheels jerked under the awkward weight, then settled. Elle hauled the cumbersome wagon out past the other side of the pier, between thickening vegetation, past the shifting, seeping lowland, and finally into the water. Before she could lug the last load, she made out a whistling. It was Monty, unusual for him to be up and about so early, especially after last night's bender.

He spoke first. "The hell you doin' up so early?"

She stared at him dumbly, unable to formulate a sentence.

"Is it Billy?"

"What? What about Billy?"

"I always knowed how he did you. Seems to me we all did. Sonofabitch. Heard the ruckus last night."

The sky was a dense green, palms outlined in black. Monty looked up. "Nevermind. Your business if you want to keep 'im. Got plenty concerns of my own." He looked at her with tenderness then said, "Storm comin', for sure. Gotta get a move on."

A door slammed softly, causing Elle to jump and drop the cart handles. Monty eyed her, frowning. But soon his attention was diverted to the singer who had tiptoed out in a bias-cut, flesh-colored slip, wearing his one good pair of shoes.

Monty smiled and Elle, grabbing her chance, snatched the handles and pointed the cart away, a posse of flies humming in the air above. She glared at Monty then shushed him, placing her forefinger to her lips and pointing up to her small window as if to warn him against waking Billy. He nodded, probably pleased to return his attention to the half-clad singer.

Partway to water's edge, Elle heard something gaining on her, breathing heavily. It was Sheila.

"Jeez, Elle, will you let me help you?" The edge of a crab trap was plainly visible, peeking from beneath the cover. "Don't need to set these. Mostly be closed over the next month. They might even wash away in the storm."

"Not likely." Do I have to explain myself, even to the second cook? "Good chance to lay in a store of food. Now get off with you. Not revealing my secret crabbing places. G'wan. Git."

"C'mon, Elle, you gotta get going. Last ferry leaving early. Radio from the Coast Guard says so."

Elle nodded, and finally Sheila turned and left.

Struggling with her load, heavier with each pull, Elle pushed her way across the spongy bog toward the water. As she moved deep into the underbrush, behind a thicket of vine-strangled scrub, bloated green horseflies dove at her head. Her marrow vibrating inside her bones like jelly, she inched out as far as she could with the last three traps. Finally, she used a pole to maneuver them toward the mangrove, where they sank, one by one. Up to her waist in water, Elle finally crawled back up the bog and looked toward the lodge. No one was about. She wedged the duffel and gunny tightly into the tangled roots of the tallest mangrove tree, holding on to a chain that she placed in the tangle of branch, the green overgrowth providing a disguise.

The ferry sounded its first warning, and Elle raised herself from the brush, as if from a stupor. Instinctively, she stood ready to run back to the pier and help with the parcels and ladies' bags, to see to it that everyone had snacks and nothing was left behind. But, fearful of anyone seeing blood on her that she hadn't cleaned, she sat back down in her spot on a log. A small lizard sat next her, undisturbed, and Elle was grateful for its company. She hung her head, willing away images from the previous evening. Billy was gone. What was at the bottom of the bog was something else, something entirely different.

The sky was dark, not a breath of air, and she made out sounds of the previous night's partygoers speaking sharply, all commenting on the weather and the drop in barometric pressure. The day felt like it was suffocating a body, and the whole island was silent; even the insects stopped buzzing. Elle watched the crowd move toward the pier, pulling trunks, hauling sacks. She sat on a large, porous limestone perch, looking through the lace curtain of leaves and ripening berries, her whole body heaving.

For the second time in as few hours, Elle doused her entire self with water, trying to wash off the stench, disregarding the raw holes where bugs had taken chunks of her, scratches from Billy, and the great gashes on her thigh and hand that now constantly throbbed. She kept moving, as if constant activity could renew and freshen her blood.

The wind started and the forest began to breathe, the water swelled and the ferry captain yelled something into the megaphone. As more scurried onto the pier, a sharp jag of fear coursed through her. *Where was Mrs. Rowlands?*

After inspecting her clothes and arms for blood, she combed her fingers through her hair and felt no clumps. She thought she looked decent enough to emerge, although the air was so sodden her hair must look like a thicket of spur. She tied a damp kerchief on her head and trooped out, leaving the cart hidden in the wood. Where did all these people come from? Elle forgot how many there were, as many had arrived from further inland, until the Captain refused to take any more; the ferry was over capacity. Elle recognized the pastor and his wife come to have words with the owner, till they heard he had left the night before. Pastor and his wife finally departed the pier, a small crowd of people trailing behind them, probably taking refuge in their home, further inland by the church.

Monty, his face dark and worried, spotted her and waved for her to come aboard. Elle wondered why it suddenly was such an urgent thing to get moving. She ignored his expression, waving back at him as if she didn't know what was going on and that he wanted her to evacuate. But he was too busy with his duties to take time to convince her, and anyhow, he knew how stubborn she was.

Relief pushed through her body as swells of waves seemed to be sifting the terror away. With no desire to leave, she watched the heavy ferry bob up and down, the horn at last trumpeting their departure. Finally the ferryboat was on its way to disappearing. The wind blew, then stopped, then blew again, and there was no doubt a bad storm was rising. Elle hoped they would be well out and on their way, too far to think of doubling back. And maybe, if it came to that, the storm would take her too, floating her on the great dark waves, over the edge, off the side of the world.

Unbidden thoughts of Dog came to her. If only she had Dog. They would run through the woods, back to the lodge. Dog would gaze upon her, his velvet eyes filled with love. The more she thought of Dog, the less she minded that Billy was somewhere at the bottom of the bog, the water rising and slamming through the traps.

14

The trudge back to the lodge was slow, her leg dragging. Although she feared permanent damage if she put any force to it, she could not shake off her practical nature. She mourned the loss of the large cart more than the revulsion of what had been in it, and made it halfway to the lodge before turning back to get it. Back to the spot where Billy lay tangled in the weeds. She finally spotted it by the milk paint that glowed an unnatural green, making it easy to find. After struggling to pull it through the boggy soil, Elle finally reached the lodge and found that the shutters were nailed on tight and the heavy chain lock was fastened. She dug out her key and unbolted the chain, but instead of going inside, she sat out on the porch steps, watching the grim sky settle like a dark angel on its haunches, waiting to strike. The place spooked her. The lodge looked forsaken and abandoned, and the surrounding grounds seemed about to shrink. The wind blew heavily, then slowed. Soon a low whistling began, then gaining and growing more shrill, almost as if the train itself was coming to No Name.

Extra kerosene was stored in the pantry by Elle's small room, but it wasn't need for supplies or fear of the wind or the lodge being close to the water that drove Elle back out to that porch landing. It was dread of nailed shutters and being shut in for hours on end. She had no desire to go into her small, blue room, with the smell of bleach and traces of blood and brain that were lodged in the cracks of the tiles, the baseboards, and the walls; so thick they would never wash out. Desolation hit Elle as she again thought of Dog and wondered if another would come out of the brush and began to call out into the wood.

She moved out to the trashcan, lifted the lid, tossed in the bundle of Billy's clothes, and covered them with newspapers to get the fire started. But she spied something just as she was ready to light the kerosene soaked rag and drop it into the trash. With a long stick, she fished out a bright white paper that looked official, like it was telling her to pay it some mind. In the center of the paper was a tight wad of cash, bound with a rubber band. She placed the bills in four piles of a hundred dollars each—more money than Elle had ever seen in one place. She didn't want it, gave herself over to thinking on how Billy's death would come to mean a profit to her, and knew that every time she saw a piece of that money or what it brought her, she would be killing him all over again. So, she dropped the bills back into the barrel, refusing to think too hard on it. Then she lit the rag and pitched it in. The rag sputtered, but much of what was in the barrel was wet, so the fire didn't catch on right away, and Elle looked around to the captive land, the storm about to take it. Panicked and anxious when the fire began to take hold, she reached in and grabbed for the cash, snatching at the bills as they did a frenzied dance around the barrel. As the fire began to spread, Elle pulled at her damp shirt, wrenched it off, and held it over the top to suffocate the fire. Standing over the barrel on tiptoes, naked from the waist up, her face charred and hair singed, she dug at the debris, letting out breath each time she snatched a bill, finally gathering more than half, the last few too burned to be of any use. This time, Elle poured kerosene into the barrel and stepped well away, imagining what anyone would see if they came upon her—a bloodied and blackened half-naked woman clutching at flames and gazing into a pot of fire. When little but ash remained, Elle felt the first drops of rain.

15

Late afternoon, the wind picked up plenty and rain began to lash diagonal, carrying with it sand that wanted to scour skin from flesh. Elle wandered out, a lone figure on the landscape under black clouds so low she feared they would corkscrew her up and away.

Although far from the shoreline, Elle was spooked by a surge of foam from a wave that crept toward her like a rabid phantom, inching closer, till it seemed it would finally swirl around her ankles like a watery snare and rush her out to sea when darkness came. Just before making for the dreaded lodge, Elle remembered the chickens in the pen and quickly corralled Charlie the rooster, a couple of hens, and six newly hatched chicks, bringing them all into the lodge, happy for the company.

Palms swayed, then whipped out to blackness and Elle heard a rush and lashing noise that pushed her up the stairs of the lodge. She finally bolted the front door and lit a lamp. Although she knew better than to waste fuel, she could not bear the darkness in this place and knew she only had to make it through one single night. She darted past the silvered mirror, not daring to look, and slipped on something, falling over her own feet, her leg too weak to right her before the lamp went out.

Matches. Where were the matches? Elle saw shapes everywhere, unable to make them out, and the noise from the winds in a thousand shrieks slammed under cracks in the frame, through keyholes and loose boards. The lodge was bolted into concrete throughout, but something, from somewhere outside, was banging against the side of the house. It was the cart! The damn cart she had carried Billy's body in, banging hard against the one spot that sounded in danger of giving way—as if it would finally have its revenge. Again Elle leaned on what she thought was a counter but was the edge of a chair. It quickly slipped and she fell painfully on her knees, felt something pull in her leg, and knew somehow that it would never again be quite right.

She crawled to the door she knew so well—the pantry—and pulled at the gingham fabric lining the shelves. Jars and boxes crashed down on her and she felt around until she finally found a box matches and lit one on the baseboard. Weeping silently with relief, she gathered six lamps and lit them all, placing them in the corners of the room. In here, the air moved not an inch, but outside, all around her, the demons struggled, sucking in breath, trying to find their way to her.

Throughout the night, the lamps remained lit, but Elle, fearful of what might be lurking behind the door, refused to enter the small blue room. She moved a chair in the center of the large ballroom and sat, alone. Finally, sometime in the middle of the night, everything became quiet, but the ringing in her ears remained. Elle refused to move, not even getting up to relieve herself, wedging a chair against the door to the blue room when the noise started up again. She tried to pray but had no talent for worship of anything but the pure forces of nature, denying the comfort of a god in which so many found a measure of solace.

Sometime before first light, a mighty crash and roar roused her from her stupor as she sat in the small chair, and it seemed to her that the winds were crying now, weeping as if remorseful for their angry outburst. Rain lashed the trees, the roof pounded, until the storm finally lost heart and dropped torrents of water and completely saturated the small island before departing.

Despite the howling winds and water swirling about the lodge, Elle knew the back of the storm had been broken. Desperate to escape the stench of iron and bleach that suffused her nostrils, she unscrewed first one bolt, than another. She stopped to gather her courage, waiting to hear anything from the other side. When only a whimper greeted her, she removed the heavy panel and opened the door.

16

Although No Name Key suffered little from the storm, the island was profoundly altered — more desolate after sloughing-off rickety structures, small trees and bushes, and flinging them out to sea. Elle grabbed an oversized umbrella from the hallway stand to use as a cane and circled the lodge, her stiff and sore leg sinking into soggy ground. A felled branch lay across the roof of the lodge, another in the landing. Denuded palms lay twisted and broken.

Out back, the lodge's store of crab and lobster pots had mostly disappeared, blown away into the night. The cart was gone. But the worst was the shed roof, in tatters, bits of it marking a pathway to the pier. A couple of vacation cottages belonging to patrons of the lodge had lost strips of tarpaper, but all in all, not nearly as bad as it could have been. Still, this would certainly mean that workers would soon be about, coming to fix the place, nosing into her business.

She loaded the small hand pump into a wagon and pulled it toward the pier. No telling what shape her unfinished house would be in. Might not even be standing, but even if it were, it was bound to be full of water that would need pumping.

On the walk to the pier, it looked lighter, as if a madman had pruned the trees, partially cleared the land, leaving stumps and odd configurations behind. Despite the thinned foliage, air refused to circulate. High, dark water swelled, the surface so black it looked like an oil slick, lapping at the desolate shore.

Elle put pressure on her leg, testing it, and it seemed to hold well enough, but still, she kept the umbrella. Moving awkwardly out to the pier, wagon in tow, she put off checking Billy in the traps, although she feared he had become dislodged in the storm. *Now is the time to do it. Now that no one is about.*

At the very least, she had to fish the duffel and gunny out of the water, take the boat out as far as she could, and dump his last remains overboard. If she could locate the crab traps and they were still intact, she would let them be for a while. So long as they stayed down and out of sight, she would leave the crabs to their feast. In just a few days, nothing of Billy would remain. In times past, Elle would stuff chicken backs into the traps to lure the crabs and it worked so well that she knew to pull them out quick. After more than a couple of days, crabs would begin to feed on each other. The chicken bones would be gone, floated away, picked clean of gristle and marrow plucked out by delicate pincers. Elle imagined the spiny discs, hollow, floating on waves, dolphins jumping at them, seabirds diving.

Once at the pier, she was relieved to find that someone had properly moored the small boat she sometimes used to haul supplies from Big Pine, and it seemed to have suffered no damage whatsoever. But Elle's head kept turning back to the mangroves as if her neck was wound on a spring. No use putting it off; she had to go and check. But it was as if a magnetic force prevented her from moving to the dark spot, her breath shallow and labored when she eyed it under her lashes.

I'll go soon enough, she thought, convincing herself that she needed to survey what harm had befallen the groves she tended for the hermit. But first, she would check on her concrete shell, knowing that if she could help it, she would never spend another night in the haunted blue bedroom at the lodge. Nor would she clean it, not even one last time, until someone was in the building with her.

Winds finally started up again, moaning soft and low, then water began coursing from the sky in a steady stream, the ground already a sodden, sorry mess. Elle hobbled painfully to her small, unfinished house behind the clearing, cursing her luck for having ever met Billy Woodman. No way was he going to haunt her small bit of paradise, lurking underwater, waiting to pounce. She had followed him wherever his whims took them both, shoring him up for the better part of her adult life. And when she finally found a way out, he would not let her be, following her to the first place where she felt safe. *I'll be damned if I'll carry him into eternity with me, letting his spirit take over what his fists had done while he was alive.* "You didn't finish the job, Billy Woodman," she muttered under her breath. "I turned the tables on you."

The concrete husk was standing, filled with water, and Elle was sorry that she hadn't managed to finish it before the storm. A roof would have saved her from having to pump out water, but she had longed for the shiny enamel sink she saw in a catalog left by one of the women guests at the lodge. She should have realized she was playing against time. Anyone with the sense of a snail could have predicted this would befall her. The shell was intact though, not a bit of damage, though it seemed a tad closer to water's edge than before the storm.

After trudging back to the lodge for buckets and a shovel, she made out the wretched cries of Charlie the rooster and his hens still trapped inside the small supply room. Charlie and the hens had made a mess of it, suddenly coming to life when she removed the shutters to let light in the room. Once she opened the door, the gang made a break for it, but she managed to stop the chicks from moving out. She chased the rooster, who screamed bloody murder whenever she got near, the two hens flapped their wings, shrieking. Once she got the chicks into a deep basket, the hens followed their tender chirrups, cawing, lurching, and bobbing, with Charlie following close behind. This unlikely procession cheered Elle as he brought her mottled family to their new digs.

Gathering up twigs and fallen bark, she corralled the little bodies in and fed them beans and rind from the lodge's supplies. The chicks began to chirp louder when she spoke to them and moved a finger back and forth, which they eagerly followed with their whole bodies. The parents stayed close, pecking at food. Fresh water was just below the limestone, and she filled a shallow basin, placing it in the center of the chicks. She laughed as they launched their small bodies into the water, splashing and cooling down. She moved quickly and placed a fallen palm branch over half the corral to keep the sun out.

Elle knew that feeding chickens was as easy as watering them. They were the garbage disposals of the Keys, making do with whatever was easy. She had always fed them rotten vegetables, sometimes clams, but keeping the shells, her secret weapon against tomato pests.

Just before giving up on ridding the tomato plants of the ever-present, irksome slugs, she scattered eggshells on the ground and made the happy discovery that slugs refused to crawl on them to get to the tender seedlings. She no longer had to lay in wait to shrivel them with salt. Just the thought of the tomato plants and the sapodilla grove caused her leg to throb.

When she rose to walk, she stumbled, losing her balance. The neck wallet swung out from her shirt, reminding her that she would need a better place to hide her money. A dangerous hole in the land, almost a foot deep, lay visible under the jumble of twigs and foliage, causing her to move carefully, testing each step. This was a perfect hiding place for the $400 dollars she rescued from the fire. She put the money in a large jar, placed the rough brown fiber from a fallen palm between the jar and the cap, and screwed the top on tight. She kept out fifteen dollars — a small fortune — a five-dollar bill, the rest in ones and twos. Mentally, she was spending the rest, replacing the damaged things in the blue room, tossing out everything when she mustered enough courage to walk through the door.

Storing her fortune at the bottom of the hole, she covered it with rocks and leaves then stepped on it until it had no give. She paced exactly nine steps to the northernmost corner of the house, not bothering to mark it anywhere but in her mind.

After making a list of chores, she convinced herself to see to the groves before tending to the most grisly business. *Plenty of time for that later,* and she pushed away the urgency nagging at her and the images of what lay beneath the tortured roots of the mangroves.

She walked mechanically into the clearing, its pathways made visible by wind-stripped trees. Closing in on the trail to the grove, Elle made out a low hiss of wind, half-expecting to hear shotgun blasts — the hermit's trademark warning.

"Just me. Comin' to tend the plants," she yelled into the air every few minutes. She closed in on the spot of loamy, worked soil, the high point of the Key and the fiefdom of the hermit, whose labored Russian name she had never mastered.

A large depression announced the beginning of the grove. The hermit had planted a gigantic ring of fast-growing palms to shield his tomato plants from harsh, salty winds. Diminishing rings of plants, each smaller than the last, formed the inner circle, with the large bull's eye of sapodillas at the center, taking in the sun. Elle imagined that it looked like a target from above, a lush and fragrant oasis, with water pumped by some ingenious contraption whose workings she could barely comprehend.

This can't be the place, not this forlorn basin. Elle, leaning against a tall, topless palm set at a peculiar angle, resisted the impulse to gasp — gone, almost everything gone, no more than a half dozen sapodilla saplings left and not a single tomato plant. Elle grabbed a handful of what remained of the soil from the devastated plantation and raised it to her nose. She tasted it, and no trace of salt in the loam told her that they could begin again. The cruel wind had taken it down, the delicate tomato plants no match for a sustained battering. Sapodillas would take time, but she knew they were only a season away from a bumper tomato crop. *No choice says it all, always tells me what to do.*

On the way back to the concrete shell, she ran down the list of supplies she would need. Next morning she would go to the hermit's trailer and leave him a note if he was out. Maybe it would cheer him up if he knew she refused to be discouraged and was ready to begin again. And then, she would find the courage to deal with Billy's remains, once and for all.

As the day waned, she trudged past the lodge, returning to her waterlogged home, realizing she would have to sleep out under the stars. She gathered what dry vegetation she could find, made it into a nest of sorts, and lay down against the outside wall of her house. Nothing stirred. The air was as silent as it had been loud the night before. Elle awoke many times throughout the night and finally first light hit sharply. With no trees overhead to soften the rays, a shaft of light pierced her closed lids.

17

When Elle awoke, she realized that only a single row of bushes and trees gave privacy from anyone on the pier. From her vantage point, she would be able to make out the comings and goings of guests, but all would still be hard-pressed to see what she was up to unless they were determined to see through the curtain of tangled branches that the storm had not taken out. The property gave her easy access to the pier, something the hermit proudly reminded her about when he handed the house to her.

Elle made her way to the lodge toolshed, found a hose, and hooked it to the pump. She primed the pump for all she was worth, hoping it would drain the water from her home quickly. Her arms were tired and sore, but after a few hours, less than an inch of water remained, and the floor was ready as it ever would be for the sun to dry it out. It may take a week to finish, but so be it; her part was over. Hungry and tired, she took no pleasure in frying and eating the plump yellowtail although it was her favorite meal. One last chore before the day is done. *One last chore, and the worst at that.*

Elle moved her head northward toward the jumble of trees that now seemed farther out, as if the land itself had shrunk from Billy's touch. No telling how long it would be before someone came to check on No Name and the lodge. Elle wondered where the storm had hit, hoping it was another empty threat that did no real damage. No ferry yet, so Elle looked out to water's edge. She had to move, and move now, if she was going to make any headway. No point in waiting for a sign, lollygagging until a second darkness came to spook her.

Suddenly everything felt urgent. No rest, not just yet. The ground oozed when she moved on it, rain still coming in fits and starts. Across the pathway, saplings she had planted were gone, one of them caught in the tree. Much of the brush was stripped of leaves, but Elle recognized the dense thicket she had hunkered down in the evening before the storm.

The Oolite perch was upended, almost under water, and Elle had to crouch and shimmy across the bloated landscape, distributing her weight as evenly as she could. She moved close but could not steal her way to the edge, knowing the land would give way, and she would become trapped after breaking through the fragile crust, into the stew below, down where Billy waited for her. There was still a good few yards to the knot of mangroves, impossible to know exactly where, until she was right upon it. Billy was calling her — jeering, knowing she had no choice but to answer, to get the gunny and duffel before they made their way upward, eventually floating and bobbing dockside, likely showing themselves the minute a boat came in.

When she tried to move a few more inches from shore, toward the mangroves, her elbow dipped drunkenly, plunging into the marsh. She straightened her spine, lifted her arm slowly, and slithered backward, like a snake, holding herself hard against the ground, ruddering her shoulders, until she felt solid ground beneath the muck.

Somehow, the edge of the land had dropped off, and the copse of mangroves slunk further out, creating a small, mangled island — a living gravestone — jealously guarding its single inhabitant, cut into a dozen pieces.

It was clear the only way to reach him was by boat. She would have to dig him out of there. Nothing about Billy was ever easy.

Mud stuck to her body through her clothes, and she considered peeling off the entire humid mess. But that would make her an easier target for the cloud of excited mosquitoes hovering overhead. They didn't skip a beat as she climbed into the small red boat.

No need to start the engine. She would simply row out the couple hundred feet to get to the cluster of trees. Maybe she could use the umbrella hook to fish out the two sacks.

The clump was dark when she came upon it. Trees seemed to have multiplied, huddling together for protection. The chains she tied around the trees to mark the spot were gone. Never a good swimmer, Elle feared diving to find them. She prodded around the roots. Fallen branches and decaying leaves made the tangle worse, and then she saw a chicken with a broken neck hanging from a tree branch, caught in an unnatural angle. Below the surface — the water murky beyond a half-foot in depth — thick roots, covered in green slime, made it impossible to gain purchase.

No sign of anything but the traps, still hanging in the water, tied off around the trees. Billy would be down there — she had wedged him in good — the chain probably still attached, choked in the sludge at the bottom. It wasn't deep, but Elle was a nervous swimmer, having been to a pool no more than once or twice in Boston, before coming here, and only in the water a few times in her six months on No Name.

But it was her only chance, and she had to take it. She had seen the bloated bodies of animals come back to shore after days in the water, as if drawn to secret signs that led them home; she knew that anything she got would be hard won. So she did what she knew — she tied the boat to a sturdy tree, removed all but her skivvies, held her nose, and fell in. *I'm coming for you, you bastard. I'm coming, and I ain't afraid.*

The water was warm, green, and dark. To avoid something sharp, she felt around for the thickening, felted trunks, trying not to think. Just get it done, she thought, expecting to poke into an eye, an open mouth, no longer caring what she would find. Elle groped around, always ending up in a tangle of trunk. Seconds ticked by and Elle knew she must come up for air.

A stab of light caught on something silver. It had to be the chain she had used to tie the duffel to the tree. She reached out but it slipped from her grasp. Water flooded into her nose, just enough to stop her searching and force her back up. But she had gone in deeply, at a strange angle, and her head slipped through an opening without enough room for her body to follow. Her neck was scraped, and Elle knew at once that she must remain calm, rework her movements. She felt down her neck, with both hands angled sharply, finally slipping through, forcing her way upward, moving her face into the air, breathing deeply.

Another minute to let oxygen course through her body

then back in, to the spot she thought the chain was, around the twisted limbs, moving so quickly that she scraped her face against something and sent up a bubble of shock when she felt the duffel, attached to something else. The chain was caught in a large root, the only reason the duffel hadn't been spirited away.

Working quickly, Elle untangled the metal and when it released, she finally pushed up, holding on to the handles of the duffel, tossing it into the boat without looking at it. It landed with a dull thud and when she finally turned, she saw the gunny sack attached to it, empty, open at the slit she had made to fit Billy's torso. It was gone, carried away by the powerful current of the storm.

Elle sat in the middle of the glade, roots holding her like a hammock, the waning sun offering no warmth. She spoke to Billy in the duffel, saying, "We meet again, Billy Woodman. However will I rid myself of you?" And she tried to push her terror of him away by speaking to him, like in the old days. The sound of her own voice soothed her. "You learned me a lot Billy, but it's time for you to finally be off." She almost laughed out loud, but a noise in the background spooked her. It was a boat, still far away but heading for the pier. Although her little rowboat was not quite hidden, they wouldn't be able to see her from where they were. Not yet.

Elle almost forgot that she had nothing on but bottoms, and when she reached for her clothes, Billy's head was laying on them.

18

As the large fishing boat made its way to the pier, Elle stashed the duffel in the weeds, fearful of sinking it again. It might be that big shot writer from Key West, a bit of a busybody, profiting from the misery around him, always digging for a good story.

She recognized the fishing rig. Captain Sandy was ex-Coast Guard, maybe sent by the owners to check on the lodge and see how it had fared in the storm.

After rolling Billy's head into the open mouth of the duffel, she twisted the chain around the tree and dropped it back into water. She scrambled into her soggy clothes, paddled back, and waited by the dock to greet them.

Captain Sandy blasted his horn twice to announce his arrival, then sent out a Morse code SOS in case anyone needed help. Her mind was empty as she paddled back to the dock at No Name.. They waited in silence while she expertly tied the boat, ignoring Jim's outstretched hand. For a moment she imagines that she spotter blood under her fingernails, but that was impossible, she had just been in water.

"Morning, ma'am. I'm Captain Sandy and this is Jim Smith. We've come in case anyone needs help."

He took in the surroundings as he spoke, looking past her to the mangrove she just left. Elle got the feeling that his was a practiced eye.

"Me and the pastor's family is all that stayed overnight, and I ain't seen hide nor hair of 'em since before the storm," she answered, speaking quickly. "Prob'ly the hermit as well. Don't suppose he would put himself in the center of a crowded boat when even the scant company on No Name is more than he can bear."

"Did you check?"

"No, sir. Did not. Thought it best to wait here. Knowed that you good folk would be here soon enough and thought t'would be better to guard against looters and the like."

"Any trouble?" Captain Sandy asked.

"No. Why?"

"You have a husband, a vet staying at a camp in Matecumbe? Billy Woodman. That right?"

"Uh-huh. Yes, sir."

"Is he here? Did he stay with you in the storm?"

"Nope. Went back in the ferry yesterday morning. Before it got bad." Elle did not trust herself to meet Jim's eyes.

"Back to Matecumbe?" Jim asked.

"Sure, that's where the ferry goes. Had to get back to work."

"Well, we're sorry to bother you, but thought we'd check up on the place."

"Not really surprised to see you, sir." Elle tried to smile

at the two of them, drumming up pity for Jim, a kindred spirit of sorts. His wife never pulled her weight, did nothing but rest, always shut in with some ailment or other. Sins of omission, sins of commission, all had same result in the end. Someone else has to do the work of two.

Imagining Jim's situation relaxed her, taking her mind off what was in front of her to do.

The captain, a stocky, weathered man, removed his cap, his eyes soft. He seemed about to reach for her hands but thought better of it. "Got something to tell you, ma'am."

"Yes..."

"Matecumbe got hit real bad. Center of the storm. Took out camps 1, 2, and 3. Not many, um, made it." He waited for her to respond.

She shook her head from side to side, trying to make sense of what he was saying.

"You mean..."

"Now, we don't know for sure, but your guy, your husband, Billy Woodman..."

She nodded yes.

"Early days yet. Bodies lost or not in one piece, There's always a chance he got lucky. But I've got to be straight with you, ma'am. I would prepare myself if I were you. As best you can. No point in false hope."

"Well, what? What should I do?" Elle looked at the ground, unsure of what kind of expression she should have. Jim bent his tall frame into her then reached out to pat her shoulder awkwardly. His head was low, hat off, as if he were already in mourning.

"You can come with us if you like, back to Matecumbe. I have to ask you, ma'am, but you should feel no shame in refusing to come. Either way, that's what we're doing." The captain stared straight at her.

"How'd you know I was here?"

"Got Jim Smith to thank for that, ma'am. Said he remembered a woman on No Name with a husband who worked in Matecumbe. Said you would likely stay put and insisted on coming for you."

"Right thing to do is all. We were heading out from Key West anyhow," Jim said, a shy, pained smile on his face, his thin arms dangling by his sides.

Damn them both. Why should I foot the bill for the saintly deeds of others?

Everything in Elle wanted to refuse. But when she looked into Jim's strained face, she knew what she should want to do. She should be desperate, hoping that her husband was safe. The "good and loyal wife" that she was would want to believe that Billy was alive and be willing to endure any hardship so long as there was the smallest chance of having him back by her side. And if he was not alive, she would wish to visit his last resting place and make a shrine of it no matter how difficult, nor what anyone advised.

But Elle had seen enough of dismembered bodies, the smell of death, and without her permission, her body began to tremble. Shivers started at her shoulders and made their way down her back, into her spine, her weakened leg throbbing.

Jim moved quickly and led her to the one, bolted-down bench that hadn't been swept away.

This time it was the captain who placed a hand on her shoulder to steady her. She cast her eyes downward, afraid he would read the fate of Billy written in her eyes.

"Noticed you were out on the boat, ma'am.'

A surge of fear stilled the trembling. These men must have done plenty of search and rescue in their day. She willed herself not to turn toward the trees that clutched Billy's remains. "Thought I might see a boat on the horizon. Looking for any sign, I guess."

"Anybody left on No Name?" Jim asked.

"You already asked me that," she snapped. "I think I told you. Just Pastor Dean and his wife." Elle caught the fear and anger in her voice and willed her tone to soften. "Good people. They took in a few stragglers."

"No one at the lodge?"

"No. Left yesterday morning, early, before the storm. Everyone else stayed at the church attached to Pastor Dean's place."

"Funny that they didn't stay at the lodge. So much more secure." Jim was eyeing her, looking puzzled.

"So fretful with my own concerns that I didn't think on how they was. Just want to go to find Billy. But I kin take you to the church. You want to come with me to see?"

"Okay, but soon as we're done, ma'am, we're heading out to Matecumbe. You can come with us if you like. Your call." Jim hesitated, looked away, then turned toward Billy's remains..

Elle spoke loudly, jarring him. "Just when we was about to have something here. A little shack I was fixin' up. For the two of us. Me and Billy."

The captain looked tired and impatient. He turned, his eyes narrowing, trying to hone in on her. "It's entirely up to you. If you want to come, you are welcome. I've got to ask, but can't promise that you will like what you'll find."

While the captain spoke, Jim placed his hand on her shoulder. He wanted her to refuse, he wanted to spare her, but she knew that she had to see this thing through—one more horrid chore, one last goodbye—though by now she felt she owed Billy exactly nothing.

They walked down the plank, through the large clearing, onto a much trodden, unpaved road. Only a few days before, the road to the church was entirely hidden, but now, she easily made out the sharp curve in the storm-sheared brush.

"Not too far. Less than a mile," she said, to break up the silence.

Small, uprooted trees were visible in the taller treetops. Tarpaper from shacks in the woods lay in odd places. Everything looked meaner, scrubbier than before the storm.

The captain, a beefy, short man, built like a boxer, swatted at a fly that landed on his neck. He finally spoke. "I don't see any good reason to go on in. Looks fine to me. Don't suppose there would be any real damage this far down." His shirt was wet down the center of his back.

Elle nodded, but he wasn't looking at her directly. He continued, obviously impatient, "We're wasting our time here, Jim. We've got more serious business to attend to."

"Just about another bit, 'round the bend," Elle said, happy they weren't chatty, didn't question her much about the previous night. She tried to flatten her hair, felt for a bandanna in her pocket but she had left it on the boat.

Finally, the small wooden church, with the house attached, came into view.

Mrs. Dean, the pastor's wife, answered the door. Her eyes immediately locked onto Elle, moving up and down her body in a practiced swivel, so thoroughly that Elle wondered if she had left a button undone. She wore a drab skirt and matching blouse with long sleeves, buttoned up to her flabby chin. For such a tiny woman, she sure had a lot of loose, red flesh and she seemed to be constantly on the move, giving her the appearance of a circling turkey vulture. Everything about her was spare. Her hair was cropped short as a man's. It almost seemed to Elle as if she was daring you to notice the bald spot on her crown, visible from almost any angle.

Mrs. Dean smiled and motioned for the small party to enter.

Elle looked around from the doorway but didn't move. She made out an inviting pair of armchairs in bright island colors, with giant leaf patterns in reds, lemon yellow, and turquoise. She had never seen such swank chairs, same size as those in the parlor at the lodge, and probably just as comfortable. Once or twice, between seasons, she had sat in those chairs at the lodge, when no one was about.

The two men stood awkwardly in the doorway. "Pleased to make your acquaintance, but sorry for the occasion." Captain Sandy extended a meaty, callused hand to Mrs. Dean. "I'm Captain Sandy, and this is my good friend and first mate, Jim Smith."

"I don't believe any of you have ever been here before." The woman managed to speak and smile at the same time.

"No ma'am, can't say as we have." The captain had his hat in his hand.

But Elle knew the comment was for her. Mrs. Dean wanted her to know that she noted Elle's absence from church services.

"Well, don't be waiting at the door. Come on in. You look like men on a mission, but surely you can spare a few minutes."

"We just wanted to check in on you and yours. This is

not a social call. We have plenty of work to attend to."

"Won't tell you word one, lest you come in, and sit for naught but a few minutes. Have a nice glass of tea. Not cold, I warn you, no ice, but a tonic nonetheless." She smiled, which caused her eyes to fall back into her head and made her teeth protrude.

The captain looked annoyed, but Jim put his hand on his friend's shoulder, patted it, and nudged him through the doorway. "C'mon, we could all use a good, tall drink."

"Don't just stand there," said Mrs. Dean, looking annoyed. "You're letting the flies in."

They stepped into the living room, and Mrs. Dean pointed to the chairs, seemingly at a loss when Jim motioned for Elle to sit. Her mouth snapped closed and she strode into the kitchen, calling Elle in after her. "Come on, missy. Come help me get these two a drink."

Jim spoke, surprising Elle. "I'll be in to help you, ma'am. This here lady's been through enough for one day." He looked at Elle directly but spoke in a loud voice, "And has many a mile to go before the day is out. I suppose she needs rest more'n all four of us combined."

Somehow, his kind words were almost too much to bear. Elle felt suddenly tired, her leg began to throb, her hand hurt, her face felt hot and flushed.

The captain turned toward her. "When was the last time you saw Billy?"

"Oh, he was getting ready to board the ferry. Little bit the worse for the previous night's festivities, I'm afraid."

"Did you see him off?" This was the second time the captain asked.

They returned with the drinks before Elle could answer. Jim handed her a tall, pink glass, and Elle nodded at him, then to Mrs. Dean.

Mrs. Dean spoke, "Pastor and our three guests drove out only a couple of hours ago. People were from somewhere up north, staying at No Name Lodge for fishing."

The Captain interrupted her. "Why didn't they ride the storm out at the lodge? Didn't hear your answer. With all due respect, ma'am, this place is much less sturdy than the lodge."

"Lodge too close to the water is why. Dangerous." Elle spoke out before the pastor's wife had a chance. All three looked at her. "I mean, I didn't offer to let them stay because I thought they would be better off further inland." Elle had feared that someone would bring up this question, in fact had agonized about it, having been well drilled in hospitality, trained by Billy to think of him first, then the owners, then the guests. The room was silent after her outburst.

Jim put his hand on her shoulder, "You did the right thing. Must've been a fearsome time for you."

Elle caught him shoot Mrs. Dean a look of authority to snuff out any comment she might be tempted to make. Mrs. Dean looked past them. "Oh, I didn't wait for anyone to ask. Mr. Dean and I just led them here. It seemed the Christian thing to do."

"Quite right." The captain nodded gravely. "I don't suppose they will get into much trouble, but if I were you, Mrs. Dean, I would put on a big supper because I also don't expect they'll get very far. Roads are blown out not thirty miles in. The only way to get around is by boat. If anyone comes by to ask, tell them someone'll be by before week's end to see to needs for food and the like. And tell them to stay put if they live here. Otherwise they'll just cause more trouble."

"Is it bad?"

"Worst storm I ever heard of. Railroad cars blown clean off the rails. Barometric pressure lower than any ever recorded. Twenty-six point thirty-six inches, if that means anything to you. You got lucky, but not everyone can say that. Just keep them in your prayers. I'm sure they'll be needing them."

"I'll be sure to pass the word along, Captain Sandy. Tell all to just stay put," she repeated.

"Ferry service is cancelled for the time being. We'll send word when we know better. And now we must take our leave." The captain rose, followed by Jim and Elle.

"How long will we be gone?" Elle asked impatiently before she realized what the mission was. "I'm sorry." She put her hand to her mouth.

"It's okay, ma'am. Never been through this before. Bound to be a strange and scary time for you. For all of us."

The small trio made their way out and Elle would have preferred a lecture rather than the lookof pity on the older woman's face. She turned and nodded thanks, and they moved silently, bracing for the trip back and the destruction they would find.

Flies were out in droves and a hunting party formed above them. A large, blue fly dove at Elle's head and got tangled in her hair, and they had to stop and ruffle her head until it finally flew away, stumbling clumsily in the air. For all she knew, it might have been the same fly that trailed her when she took the crab traps out.

Too worn out to protect her leg, she began to hobble, tried to keep up with the men who were eager to get on with their duties. More than anything, she had to get to the lodge for fresh bandages. She felt an urgency to brush her hair and change her clothes.

19

"Hope they let us on through," Jim said.

"Course," she answered in a small voice. Her whole body was throbbing, but neither her thigh nor hand was swollen, so they weren't infected. Not yet. "Just nerves and exhaustion. Kin I beg your indulgence for one last thing?"

Jim said, "Sure," and the Captain said, "Depends," at exactly the same time.

"I want to make myself a bit presentable. Get some supplies. Can't really afford to buy anything as I go."

"We'll be at the boat," Jim said as the lodge came into view. "Take all the time you need. We'll be waiting."

The afternoon was on the wane; the sky was a peaceful, hazy blue-lavender. If the fishing boat had not come, Elle could almost have convinced herself it was any other hot September after a storm passed through.

She took the stairs carefully, once the men were out of sight. Slowly she hobbled to her old blue bedroom. The air was putrid, sour smelling. She breathed shallowly, moving quickly, opening drawers, gathering brushes, clean skivvies and bandannas for her hair. When she breathed deeply, she tasted metal. Elle followed her nose, and it led her to the horsehair mattress. When she lifted the canvas tarp, she saw that the stain had spread over the striped mattress ticking. Moist and pink, brown in the spots where blood had dried, it let off a sickly odor, and Elle wanted to drag it out back and place it next to the lavatory. She had master keys to all the guest cottages and planned to grab someone else's mattress when she returned, claiming that the storm got in through a window and destroyed their bed. *Dammit, I should have come here earlier.*

She pulled the mattress through the narrow door, grappling with its bulk, tugging and pulling it down the ramp out back to the fish butchering place. It alarmed her to see the telltale brown stains in light of day, and she was about to turn it over to hide them when she thought better of it. It was raining, and she would charge the weather with doing the work she could never manage alone. If anyone came upon it, she could claim it had gotten so wet that it would cause fungus to grow in the cabin. The entire process took no more than a few minutes. The boat horn sounded, warning her to get a move on. But this time she ignored their call. *Let them come and get her or go on alone.* She would take what time she needed to prepare for the ordeal.

At the kitchen sink, she poured peroxide on her wounds, found the first aid kit reserved for guests' injuries, and dressed her wounds properly, finally stretching bandages first around her thigh, then her hand. After pouring a bucket of water over her head in the kitchen sink, she scrubbed her scalp, face, and hands, scouring off the sweat, soot, and grime of the day. She dried her face until it shone and tied her hair back in a cheerful pink bandanna. She dressed quickly in a summer skirt and a tunic, then opened a window to air out the room as best she could. Before heading to the boat, she went to the spare cabin, the one Monty sometimes stayed in, gaining access with her skeleton key. She opened the windows, stripped the mattress of bedclothes, propped it up against a wall, and shut the door behind her. She would tell him that his was destroyed in the storm and she had replaced it with hers, always seeing to the needs of others before her own, as was her nature. On her way to the boat, she gathered three dry palm fronds, the only way to protect against bloodthirsty and conniving insects.

Light was waning when they finally set sail. "We'll be picking more up in Grassy Key," the captain said. But no one was waiting when they arrived. Elle was surprised at how few were on the water, going to claim the dead. Were they already there?

During the four hours it took the boat to get to Matecumbe, Elle's thoughts turned to the stories he told her. Stories that she later discovered belonged to other men, other wars, even. And she should have known by the way he relished telling tales of blown off arms and men screaming in agony. She should have known that he would be drawn to brutality over and over again, and that she would forgive him, turning herself into a victim, as if it could make him into the man she wanted him to be. She would take the pain and absorb it for him, and he would heal. That's what she thought back then. After they moved into their own place, she understood that she had been duped into pity for the beast that may well have been happy for a war to act out his desire to wound. Either way, he was not hers to cure, a lesson she learned late, but if she were lucky, perhaps she had learned it just in time.

She sat silent, bow side, as they passed by wrecked wharves and splintered boats, the destruction becoming more extreme the further they traveled. Empty houses canted, like hollow, bleached skulls with windowless sockets, set askew.

Once, when she looked overboard, she spotted a screen door, and later, the three of them jousted with a washing machine, pushing it out of their way with a set of oars. Jim thought it prudent to warn her of what she would be seeing. "Bodies, ma'am. I got to tell you. It's all right if you don't recognize Billy...no matter that you could be looking straight at him...if you know what I mean. Truth be, I don't know why you should be made to go through this. Not one bit...I just don't see it."

Please, thought Elle, give me the strength to look upon more death, and severed limbs.

When Elle looked away, he continued, not caring. "If you ask me, don't even bother to look. Some things better left unseen, especially for one such as yourself, ma'am. Reckon your plate is heaped high enough right about now."

She held her head in her hands, hating him for his kind words, for making her remember when she may have been exactly the kind of woman he thought she was. Before she laid eyes on Billy.

20

A giant beam of light shone on their boat and a horn sounded. Elle couldn't see anything in the dark, the light shining in her face.

"Who goes there? This is the American Coast Guard. Identify yourself."

"Captain Sandy Jones and First Mate, Jim Smith, coming in with Elle Woodman to find Billy Woodman, Great War veteran and husband, presumed lost in the storm."

It was the first time Elle had thought of him in such important terms, and it was true. Maybe she could learn to think of him this way, lost at sea, and it would take the horror out.

"Follow this beam to dock."

"Sir? We're going to Matecumbe."

"This is the closest you will get. Soldiers are on their way tonight to start in on the cleanup operation. Docks washed out. You have permission to stay on your boat and make the trek from here tomorrow. But, only if you strictly follow our instructions. Any deviations and you will have to leave the territory. But tonight, everyone must stay put."

The Coast Guard officer spoke with finality.

Even in the dark, the land was clear and sharp, white as an exposed bone, as if the storm had plucked man's puny structures and blown them skyward, where they disappeared.

They were in Craig Key, still a number of miles from Matecumbe. Elle had an overwhelming desire to see what had happened for herself but didn't dare leave the boat. Although the dock was full, the night was oddly silent, broken only by murmurs, whispers, and the occasional whine and cry of a child.

The pier seemed cockeyed, leaning a bit toward one side. A patchwork of furniture was drying out just beyond the shore, in open air. After an hour of no one around, Elle decided to leave the boat and venture inland to see the damage for herself, but as soon as she exited the boat, the Coast Guard was upon her.

"Ma'am, we got no time to be policing you. Tomorrow — you can get to the place tomorrow."

"And what place is that, exactly? Matecumbe?"

"No, ma'am. Not much left there, and what's there is not fit to be seen. Moving everything here. About a mile down that path, bodies will be on the bank for identification, if possible. God be with you, ma'am."

From behind her, Jim called out, "Sir."

The Coast Guard stopped.

Again, "Sir, do you happen to know anything about a ferry, The Key Wester? Left No Name Key, September 2, early in the morning, bound for Matecumbe. Haven't heard word one on the fate of the voyage and the people on it."

"No, sir, but again, check in the morning. Should be more news then. Now…good night."

He touched his cap and Elle understood that there was nothing more to do but wait on the boat until morning.

With Jim sitting next to her on deck, them both slapping at insects, Elle realized she had worn her best things for nothing. Still, it was good to be sitting in the moonlight, next to a decent man who had concerns about her well-being. She hit something biting her wrist, and he smacked at his leg. Elle handed him a stiff palm frond. "I brought these. Nice and dry. Nothing else works."

"Not true," he said and went below decks, coming back with a couple of black metal bowls. Then he poured a bit of oil into one and lit it, sending a flame into the air, followed by heavy smoke. Captain Sandy had made himself a nest and began to snore in between smacking at insects. Jim picked up a tarp and covered his friend's feet.

"He might get hot, but better'n being eaten alive." He moved a pot next to the captain and placed the other behind himself and Elle. A steady stream of thick smoke curled upwards. "Confuses the little so-and-sos," he chuckled. "Feels good to win one round. All you can ask for sometimes."

"More than you get most times," she replied, and they nodded at each other in the dark, then both spoke at the same instant about how they came to be in this crazy part of the world.

"Georgia. Never been to Georgia," she said, and the last thing Elle remembered was something about an orchard and a barn with cats.

She awoke to the sound of a child crying against the backdrop of a pink sunrise. She had a soft blanket under her head, her shoes were off, her feet covered by a tarp. When she looked for Jim, he lay curled up near the bow. The captain had come up from his quarters and nodded at her, kicking at Jim to wake up. They breakfasted on a loaf of bread and a couple of pickled eggs. Jim handed her a glass of water to wash it down, and the sounds of people stirring began.

They sat, silently chewing for a few minutes, Elle embarrassed at the two men observing her at such close quarters. The captain knew someone inland and left early to see how the family had fared in the storm.

A very young soldier walked down the pier and clapped his hands.

"Gather round. I got news for anyone of you waiting to hear on casualties." He clapped his hands again, and boats began to creak as people, wrapped in shapeless, soiled cotton and all manner of dress, moved out on deck. About a dozen women and children had somehow made it here. Some looked so dusty and worn-out that they could have have walked from Key West.

"We're doing the clean up now, should have news soon, but may take another day or so. Can't promise anything."

Jim volunteered to help without being asked, and Elle offered, too, but before the soldier could respond, Jim nodded to him and the two men went off down the wharf.

When they returned, the soldier spoke. "Didn't realize you're the wife of one of the vets and come to find out about him, ma'am. Can't let you into Matecumbe. Sorry."

"But surely you could use a good pair of helping hands?" Elle asked, as the men's gazes moved to her bandaged hand. "Oh, please," she said. "This ain't much."

Jim nudged the soldier.

The soldier replied, "Policy. Can't have families of the men doing the dirty work. Not good for anyone."

"Mighty quick to form policy," Elle said.

Jim spoke to Elle, ignoring her last remark. "If you wait here, I'll find out what I can, and then we can take you back tonight. If Billy Woodman's here, I'll find him. I promise you that. Maybe you can help with kids or something here."

Elle didn't know why he was being so kind. He didn't owe her anything. He was no relation of hers. He tossed her a small, silk bag with a drawstring. "Here's the key to below decks. Keep it locked if you leave the boat. Bound to be thieves about. Take a load off and get some shut-eye if you like. Captain won't be back till nightfall. Told me so before he went."

Before Elle had a chance to argue, he said, "Only key there is, so better be around and about when I get back, probably sometime after sunset."

Elle turned away when the soldier — a boy barely out of short pants — stared at her with open pity. She turned to the women, "So whatcha got to eat?" When no one offered anything, Elle spied a few fishing rods. "Hey, kid." She aimed her words at a gangly boy in a pair of bright red girl's shorts. "You look like you might know yer way around a fishin' pole. Biggest fish gets this." She tugged out the cloth wallet she wore on a string around her neck, pulled out a dollar bill, and held it up for them to see. Three boys and two girls jumped out of the boats.

Elle handed out a couple of poles and a few of them had their own. "Let's get this thing moving," she said. "There'll be plenty of hungry men about in no time. Be a good thing to have something for them to eat." Two of the women nodded at her, the younger of them missing her front teeth. *Too young to be so worn out,* Elle thought.

"Seems to me we number a good dozen. By tonight, we

may be twice that, so anyone who has anything, be much appreciated to toss some into the pot. Tonight we break bread together in a fish fry up. Plenty for everyone if the kids do the job. Nothin' to be done to hurry the men's job any faster." *Or any easier*, she thought.

Elle, energized by the activity, lost herself in gathering large pots and making a makeshift cutting place. She gave one of the girls a bit of money for some good bread and a few dozen eggs. "And get me some potatoes and whatever greens, like celery or onions, if they have it. What the dilly-o," she said, and gave out another quarter for treats for the kids. "Spend it all," she said, "on whatever you like, candy, anything."

She took the little girl's hand, placed a quarter into it, and closed her small fist around the money. The little girl began to walk away, her step somber, as she said, "Yes'm."

"You," Elle said looking at the older girl, then turned to who must be her mother, "Can you go with her?" The woman stared through Elle but finally agreed to go with her. The woman ran a hand through sweat-dulled gray hair and, without exchanging more words, she turned and left, the two girls trailing behind.

Elle did not quite know what to do with herself. She was used to scrubbing and hauling, mending and sweeping and slicing, cleaning out things all day long. When the cabin was in shape and no one yet back from their expeditions, she lay out on the boat. She had almost convinced herself that she really was expecting news about poor Billy.

By early afternoon, they returned. One of the boys had a couple of snappers. "Not bad, enough to start the soup, not mor'n that. You gotta do better'n that," she said, and sent him on his way. "Go to where there's shadows and a big show of rock. They'll be taking their rest in the shade, same as any creature. Won't be able to resist the promise of food."

She tossed the fishes into the pot, head and all, after cleaning them—one of her secrets for a flavorful broth. When the double gas burner was crowded and steaming, Elle turned it off, lay down, and fell into a blissful afternoon nap, awakening to the sound of children talking over her. They had bags of fish and vegetables, and she shared some of the soup as a starter with two other women who then began to chop fish up, placing large chunks into the broth. Elle showed them how to mix the flour with a bit of egg and place it on the broth to cook into dumplings. "Long as you save some of the starter, you can feed great masses of people. Just keep on adding stuff, flavor stays. Fishes almost seem to multiply. Learned that somewhere."

21

T he children ate and, by afternoon, some were down and napping. The two women were finally able to get some rest, though one of them whimpered in her sleep.

Jim returned before nightfall, and soon the captain followed, a couple of young soldiers in tow. Hollow-eyed, they refused to eat at first, and Elle wondered what they had seen. She coaxed them to have some food, and one of them exclaimed, "What did you put in this, Missus?"

"Good, ain't it," Jim said. "Elle is considered the greatest cook on No Name."

"And at times the only one," she mumbled.

No one demanded news from the soldiers. No one asked what they expected or when they would hear word. They let the men settle down to eat. The soldiers looked like faraway children, already gone somewhere else.

After sweet treats were given to the kids, the sky darkened and stars hung low in the sky. A soldier looked around, taking in the women and children who seemed just as intent on watching his every move. It seemed as if he had just remembered why he had come.

He vaulted out of the boat and stood in the center of the wharf. Standing tall, he ran the whole of his palm back to the front of his scalp and raised his head up. "Listen up, everyone. We got some of the bodies laid out, more coming in the morning. There's no other way of saying this. Whomever we haven't found by now is not likely to be in a fit state to identify. After tomorrow, you'd all best be on your way. No use staying."

Captain Sandy joined him, adding, "Mr. Rien will be needing this wharf back soon, so we must ask you good folks to be off by noon tomorrow. Good luck, and may God be with all of you."

Everyone began to rustle. A voice yelled after the departing men, "Hey. How many bodies do you have?"

The soldier turned his young, weatherbeaten face toward the boats. His lips barely moved as he responded, "Don't rightly know how to answer that," and Elle envisioned Billy's severed limbs floating in the crab traps and hung her head, then looked to the soldier's hollow eyes, beginning to grasp the tremendous damage that had been done.

Soon, all was silent, until finally Captain Sandy said that he was going back to his friends' place a mile in on Craig Key to comfort the widow and make funeral arrangements for her husband, lost in the storm. "Least I can do," he said. "He was Godfather to my kids."

Jim and the captain went off together for a powwow, and when Jim returned alone, he told Elle a ferry leaving at noon the next day could take her back to No Name.

She nodded, strangely sad to be leaving this unholy place. Exhausted, she began the cleanup, but Jim stopped her. "I'll be taking care of this. Plenty waiting for you to do in days to come, I'm sure. And pardon my boldness, but I'll not take no for an answer."

When she settled back on the lounger, he reached for the wadded up sheet he had placed under her head the night before then seemed to hesitate. He said, "Below decks there's a good bed and a light. Sandy's wife liked to read movie magazines. Ever seen one?" Elle couldn't make sense of what he was saying until she remembered magazines the guests had left. "Go have a look-see. You'll be fast asleep in no time."

Elle wasn't sure if the captain would approve, but Jim was tender, determined to make her comfortable. Elle smiled, remembering the pastor's wife's expression when Jim made her hand Elle a glass of lemonade.

She did not want to seem ungrateful but wasn't much on narrow spaces and had to fight feelings of being closed in, preferring to sleep in the open when she got the choice.

"Matches in a pouch, down to the right side of the stairs," he said as he pulled her up by the hand and gently propelled her toward the opening in the deck.

She pulled her wrap around her, even though it was a steamy evening, and then swung down the compact opening, down the short staircase, feeling her way till she located the leather pouch of matches. She lit one on her shoe and it flared, lighting up the cozy space, illuminating an ornate kerosene glass lamp. She was expecting tight quarters but came onto a clean, narrow bed with cheerful orange and green bedding and a scalloped, green- shaded lantern on a teak trunk, with a stack of magazines and a parade of books in bright paper jackets. Books she had never heard of, but ones she was able to read though she hadn't done so in a long time. *Stamboul Train* by Graham Greene, *Brave New*

World and another entitled *Christmas Pudding*. None of these interested her, but anything was better than lying alone, staring up at the ceiling.

She felt around for the movie magazines, turned up the flame, and located a small stack. What she saw immediately startled her. *True Detective, Telling Tales,* and *Detective Story Hour*. She had no idea that such things existed, and she began to read. *Cord of Death* absorbed her for a while, but she kept searching until she found an island adventure story that made her long for a life of travel, free from worry. Then she went back to the strange story of the supernatural. It seemed to her that she might be a little of all the characters in the story and then it didn't matter anymore. She began to relax, wondering why anyone would fool around with the occult in the first place, and would the girl be rescued in time.

The bed was too neatly made to disturb, so Elle lay on top of the coverlet, not wanting to leave any mark. She discovered an overhead compartment stuffed with pillows, a small, folded sheet, fine nightgowns, and gossamer hankies that seemed made of embroidered fairy wings.

After much time of no movement or sound from the upper decks, she removed her clothes, folded them neatly on the floor, and picked up another magazine. Before she finished reading the second story, sleep began to overtake her.

Sometime later, she blew out the light. She awoke to a feeling of tremendous emptiness, as if she were inside a vast rising wave, and imagined the sea rushing in through the portholes. She heard something stir, closing in on her, then made out the silhouette of a man. Intuitively, she pretended to be asleep and her eyes, now adjusted to every nuance of the darkness, recognized the unmistakable shape of Jim. A feeling of warmth settled on her face as she felt his direct stare.

He leaned in closer, tucking the sheet around her feet, stopping to look one last time, making Elle aware that the sheet no longer covered her legs. Every part of her wanted to pull him down, topple him onto the bed, finally, and for once, not to be alone. But she waited, waited for the waves to carry Billy out, waited for the crabs to begin feeding and finally eat each other, destroying all evidence, their bodies absorbing his, taking everything with them. Waited for Billy's torso to join the legions of others washed away in the storm. Waited for the hermit to finally let her stay, his signature on the line, the sink installed, the guests fat and happy and drunk, the owner's wife running a white glove over the baseboards and handing her the narrow pay packet.

She opened her eyes, and Jim seemed in some sort of pain until he realized that she was watching him. Elle reached for his hand and he said nothing, just moved to the bed, his head grazing the narrow shelf above her head. He laughed nervously when he lay next to her, so she placed her hand over his mouth to silence him then climbed over his long body, reversing their positions. She lay straight over his rigid form, pressing her body into his, feeling his slender cock stiffen under her, and the rhythmic intensity of their breathing swell and rise. They rocked together slowly, prolonging the crush of pleasure, and Elle pinned his hands to the mattress, intuitively knowing that he would appreciate a woman capable of decision and action as much as she needed a man who could be still. And for a moment she was the pirate in the sea adventure she had read and he a prince she had rescued from the deep. When they rolled over, she smiled at him in the dark, the first calm smile she had felt in as long as she could remember. She reached for one of the owner's flimsy hankies to mop his face and could have sworn that she was wiping tears from his eyes. She felt for his hand and held it tight, the hand that she would push away when first light came.

When morning came she didn't have to send him back up the narrow stairs; he was already gone. He knew better than to ask if she was all right. He knew, somehow, that she would not appreciate a show of concern. More, she needed the small bit of time to savor the comfort and warmth that she felt. And it seemed for all the world that it was right, the one true action in this place of sorrow — a fizzle of joy in the torrential grief that would drown the place, repeatedly, in days to come.

22

By early morning, Elle had rendered the small cabin crisp and tidy, returned the detective magazines to the table, shook out and smoothed the covers on the bed.

The rotten smell that hung in the air the night before had inched its way into her clothes and hair, impossible to avoid. It was as if a sewage vein had opened and someone poured sulfur over it.

Jim was on deck, and he and Elle greeted each other carefully. He seemed about to speak but she silenced him with a downward wave of her hand then busied herself by getting provisions left over from the previous evening's fish stew. She handed him a heel of bread and they sat side by side. Before he had a chance to speak, the boy with red shorts came to their boat. He was carrying a soiled paper bag.

"Mister?"

"Yes?"

"Got a deal to make with you."

"What kind of a deal?" Jim asked. A small boat tethered to a larger vessel knocked about, and a half dozen people began to stir.

The kid spoke in a loud whisper. "Got something you might be interested in but want to make a trade." The kid pointed to the brown paper bag.

"What you got there, kid?" Jim and Elle were up now, leaning over the side of the boat.

"Can I come onboard? Don't want my mom to see."

Elle nodded yes, and the gangly boy barreled over the side of the boat. Elle smiled as best she could, relieved for this diversion.

"I know there's going to be bodies, and my mom been getting worser and worser, smelling the air and thinking of finding father and all, if he's there."

While they spoke, a group formed on the banks. Soldiers were out, looking grim, hollowed out. The kid began to speak, speeded up, as though he couldn't get words out fast enough.

"They won't let me go to see if it's him and my mom has got to know, but they say I'm too young to go. If my dad is gone, that makes me man of the house. It's my job to have a look-see. That way she'll know for sure. I know she trusts me and if I say I seen him, she'll believe it."

"I don't see what this has to do with me," Jim commented.

"If you say I'm your kin, they'll let me go with you. It's the only way. Then my mom will stay away, see? From what I've heard of how they look, don't know what it will do to her if she sees him."

"Why not spare her and yourself? Don't neither of you have to go," Elle said to the boy.

"But please, ma'am, I got to know, too. I just gotta see for myself."

"I don't see why it's so important. All this silly..." Elle's face was set, her mouth pursed.

"Don't be mad at the boy." Jim looked at the kid, ignoring Elle. "What do you have there, son?"

The boy looked from Jim to Elle, with a bright, manic smile. "For you, ma'am. From the fishin'." He was nodding furiously. "I saved these here for you. The biggest ones."

"You should've put them in the pot. Selfish boy!"

"Elle, what are you saying? You come here for the same reasons he did. You got to see for yourself."

Suddenly Elle felt ashamed, tired of pretending that she was one of them and turned away, but she had nowhere to go. Not below decks to another man's room, nor could she turn to Jim, another woman's man. The kid looked to her then cast his eyes down.

"Take him, then," she said to Jim. "Take him and let's be done with it."

The boy took off to tell his mother a tale to stop her from coming and returned a few minutes later. Elle fumbled with her things, packing and folding and rearranging, but she had prepared it all before she went to bed the previous night.

The kid wore a fishing hat and had already changed from shorts to long pants. He waited on the wharf while Jim put a cap on and Elle vaulted over the side of the boat. Jim handed each of them a damp kerchief. The three of them followed a thickening queue into the small clearing that formed on a path away from the shoreline. A few stragglers lingered, as if in shock, handkerchiefs over their mouths and noses if they had them, hands if they didn't. The crowd marched, mostly silent, down the mucked up pathway, eyes cast downward, watching, so their shoes wouldn't get sucked off by the mud. They moved past men piling up debris—large pieces of wood, tarpaper, children's toys. A small baby's leather shoe lay on the pathway and no one said anything about it. Two rows seemed to form, parting around it, no one stooping to pick it up. After a short while, the procession grew to about a hundred men and women, a few children whining, almost too exhausted to cry.

Jim tried to walk alongside Elle, but she nudged him next to the kid and moved ahead of them both. No point in getting used to someone by her side. Besides, she didn't deserve the company, not like the kid who had a real body to find.

The pace of the crowd picked up, catching the welcome scent of smoke that came from beyond a stubby hill. Anything was better than the foul odor, unmistakably that of rotting bodies. When they got to where the smoke came from, Elle realized that there actually was no spot at all. No way to hide the evil smell, like a lavatory left out in the sun. Smoke didn't do the trick. Elle thought she spied a leg sticking out from under a shack collapsed on its side like a crushed cardboard box.

The rag-tag crowd was angry, gaining momentum, and tried to move in further, until a large guy wearing a gas mask stopped them. "If you come here in hopes of finding a loved one, you might as well get on back. Can't put this nicely, but bodies will have to be burned."

"Mister," a young man's voice rang out from the crowd. "We got a right to go in and see."

"I'm telling you, it doesn't matter what you find. Bodies splitting open from the heat, disease spreading, and you could be looking straight at your family member and not even know what you're seeing."

"So how we supposed to know if he's dead or alive?"

"Safe to say if you don't hear, you got to be prepared for the worst."

"But we were told we would have some answers," a woman yelled from somewhere in the crowd.

Elle couldn't believe what she was seeing swarming around her—boy scouts, men in uniform, Red Cross workers. And then the vets—the old soldiers always pressed to do the worst of the dirty work, not able to refuse the money, all out of luck, or they wouldn't have been here in the first place. If the storm didn't take them, then they were left to clean up the mess others had made, again, as if they were strangers brought in from another country. One that looked a lot like home, but whose comforts belonged to other men, other families. Elle heard a soft splash and saw a soldier, tears streaming down his face, pulling at a piece of what looked like a decaying arm, but Elle didn't look too close. It was no use; there was nothing more to be learned here.

When she turned to find Jim and the boy, they were lost in the ever-thickening throng, impossible to find. Everyone was the color of mud, the wreckage more pronounced the closer they got. A pile of body parts melded together, barely hidden by a broken sail someone had hastily used as a screen for the sake of decency. She thought of Billy. He never had a chance. *Still, it was him or me. And for once, it was him.* It dawned on Elle that she had done the work of the storm, the fate he tried to cheat the storm out of fulfilling.

She moved along the line now breaking up. A howl rose from a woman in a shroud, but the worst were the kids, openly staring. Images searing themselves behind their eyes, destined to return in years to come, when they felt alone, or when something let them down.

Unbidden, Elle remembered she and Billy coasting from town to town, she young and dumb enough to sit by him in his boss's new Ford, before he learned the gratification of using his God-given fists to do what his tongue had no power to achieve. And it was as if he was there—his legs, his arms—and she began to feel nothing for what was around her—the moaning and groaning, the milky eyes, the flattened features.

The boy came into view. Elle spotted him behind Jim, who had failed to scare him from trying to find his father. Elle let them alone. Maybe this will be the last time he has a man to look out for him—if only for a slender split in the universe before it stitches itself back up. He forever will be on the other side, the one to guide them now, the new man of the house. He will learn, Elle thought. He will learn to hold his counsel, keep his pain to himself till maybe he can no longer bear it.

Elle waited on the other side of the incline for Jim and the boy to come back, her words unstuck in her throat, spilling out into the air, making her just another flailing lunatic speaking to herself.

They walked toward her slowly, the kid steadying himself, and Elle knew without hearing that Jim had lied to him, told him that he had gotten word on his father, that he didn't have to search any longer. His kindness caused her to bow her head and hold fast against the gathering tears. Slowly, Jim released his arm from around the kid's shoulder, giving him a gentle push, and the kid seemed to gain in vigor, shoring himself up, as are the ways of young men, making his way to his waiting mother and sisters.

They walked the last twenty minutes in silence, back to

the dock now thick with boats banging against each other.

The sun glinted off Jim's wedding band as if to announce his departure, and the two of them nodded, having nothing left to say. Without a trace of sadness or regret, Jim said, "Ferry leaving your way in an hour and if I was you, I would get right on it. No telling how many you might have to fight for a place."

She grabbed her things from the boat. "So true, Mr. Smith. And no telling when there'll be another coming this way." She spoke in an unnaturally cheerful voice. He reached for her hand as she walked past him, but Elle pushed it away, having no stamina for a choked goodbye. "See you in the funny papers," she said, aware of how stupid this sounded, but not caring.

It turned out the boat back was not crowded at all, half-filled with somber people staring out, the sea still roiling. After a while, Elle wondered when they would get to Indian Key, but someone told her they had already passed it. She hadn't recognized it because it looked like not a single blade of grass remained on it. The rise was gone; the ground was leveled. Not a tree or a house had survived, from what she could see.

People began to murmur. A man, his bandaged arm in a sling, making his way back to Key West, told of land crabs. "They raced to me but I was holding onto a tree for dear life. Thank God, that tree held. It was growing out of coral and for all its slimness, the tree and me made it." The small crowd gathered as he continued, "Just before the big swell, land crabs raced to me. To my horror, they burrowed into all crevices of my body to save themselves, and nothing I could do about it. I was too terrified of letting go the tree."

"Read the Herald. Says five hundred or so dead.

Yesterday they said two hundred." The old man had a newspaper and everyone was silent while he read it aloud. The boat swayed and the Captain yelled, "Anyone for No Name Key?"

23

I t was still light when the boat docked at No Name Key, and Elle was the sole passenger to disembark. The lodge, once her beacon of safety, was now a place of horror. She waited until the boat was out of sight, her secretive nature asserting itself the minute her feet hit shore.

The chicks began chirping wildly when they heard her advancing toward them. She found the sack of corn she had stashed and filled their empty bowls, the noise attracting Charlie the rooster. Then the hens came running, scratching at the ground, settling in for a good long feed.

Elle counted nine steps from the corner of her concrete-block home until she spied what seemed to be the spot. She kicked at a piece of coral and it dislodged fairly easy, exposing the tight pile of small rocks she had placed over the jar. Carefully, Elle lifted each rock, and when the hole was hollow, she stuck a branch inside. Scorpions hide in piles exactly like these in the daytime, waiting for cover of night, and she wanted to let them know she was coming so they would scurry on out. She didn't want to spook them.

A half dozen pairs of leather work gloves were in the supply room at the lodge, and a good, broken-in pair sat in her old dresser, but she wouldn't be getting them any time soon. No way she was going back to that place till it was good and flush with sunshine and happy voices.

Finally, the jar came into view, and Elle pried it out, pleased that moisture hadn't gotten in and ruined the bills. After shaking it and seeing that the bills were nice and dry, she stuck it back in and replaced the stones.

The concrete flooring of the cistern seemed a natural spot to build her bed for the night. She gathered palm fronds and placed them in layers on the slab, tucking them under a tarp. Another layer of fronds, two sheets, and another waxed tarp would do well to keep water out. She burned the smudge pot low but wasn't foolish enough to think it would keep the biting insects at bay. Last thing she did before sleep was to pat the bow knife she stashed under her island mattress.

Before morning broke, she heard a noise, felt a vibration somewhere near the block of cement she lay upon. It must be some forlorn creature on the prowl.

The night was moonless, and all was still, so she settled back in, tucking her feet under the heavy sheet. One side of her neck was badly bitten and her sore hand seemed to have swollen, likely from the volume of poison injected by the swarm stalking her in the dark. The lodge almost seemed a welcoming place until she thought it through.

Memories of what she had seen of the soldier's camp at Matecumbe before the storm hit came to mind, unbidden. She recalled the flimsy tents, the heat the men suffered through, the hard labor on the roads, slinging pickaxes, pouring tar, hammering away in the blistering summer sun.

None of them young anymore, most veterans of the so-called Great War fought fifteen years before. At best, they were closing in on forty years old, like Billy, hard times pushing them even further past their prime.

Her mind turned to the smaller tents stashed in the supply room, but they were property of No Name Lodge, and she had no claim to them. Maybe she would borrow one so she could figure out how to make one of her own. Looked simple enough, and it would keep her out of the lodge till people arrived. No one would be the wiser, so long as she set it up at nightfall and got to work on her own place before tourist season started up again.

Throughout the night, she only managed snippets of sleep, finally waking to a pink and gold morning. Black rain clouds appeared as quickly as the horizon had lightened, and again the leaves didn't move an inch. This was how the Labor Day tempest had formed, but this time Elle noticed, with relief, that there was no strange, gray stillness.

Elle pushed out of her bed, reached for her knife and belt, then wandered close to the water's edge, noticing that the spongy earth was already more solid than the day before, and hopefully it would be even drier tomorrow. Silver driftwood had tumbled inland, looking like a game of jacks played by giants.

Great hanks of seaweed lay about, spit up by waves, and Elle dragged out her tarp to gather as much as she could manage. She was thinking ahead to the tomatoes, and how lucky she was, for a change, to have all this fertilizer coming to her.

Her ankle caught on a felled tree branch jutting out from a tangle of debris. The force sent her reeling to her knees, landing her on remnants of coral. She righted herself and leaned back on her haunches, sniffing the air like a dog, taking in a broken sail caught at an unlikely angle on the disheveled beach.

Although her leg hurt, Elle saw bounty all around her — coconuts, palm fronds and plant leavings that would be useful to cushion her home, keep the insects and the weather at bay. It had been almost a week since the storm passed, and she could sense that movement was afoot. She ignored the large, ragged scrape on her knees and sat still, mapping a course to Billy's remains.

A noise disturbed her and she tensed, as if being watched. She crouched lower, feeling for her bow knife. A low thud sounded from high in the branches. Perhaps it was only a bird, returned to an empty nest. Like her. Then she heard it — a raspy, guttural yowl straight above her in the branches, something she had never really liked, preferring the company of dogs. She could ill-afford the luxury of a cat, but the creature's pitiful yowls grew more desperate, as if sensing it had been spotted. She left it where it was and rose to her feet, mapping a path to another large bunch of seaweed.

The cat suddenly leapt out of the branches, landing on Elle's head, scratching her face. She swatted at the thing and it crashed by her feet, unable to move its legs. She walked over to it, wondering if she should kill it to put it out of its misery. But it looked up at her, almost angry, and something in its demeanor made her laugh. She had to admire the arrogance of the thing yelling at her when it was totally at her mercy. It was small and bright orange, with one orange eye, the other gone, a gelling wound in its place. It yelled at her again, demanding food and care, all the while hating her. She picked it up, stared in its face, and plunked it into her sack, where it briefly fought before settling into a labored sleep, its breath rattling from a lung infection or some other internal injury, no doubt. The water had coughed up this little cat like an ugly spitball. She leaned over the small body trapped in her bunting, her hair spilling over him, causing him to shiver. Her hair was the same orangey-brown as his fur, the color of dying seagrape leaves.

24

She made out another noise in the distance, but this time it was no cat. A bounce of fear pinged her till she heard her name being called.

"Elle Woodman. You there, Elle?"

Elle peered out from the nest of storm wreckage to see the pastor's wife, Mrs. Dean, her two boys in tow, yelling into the tangle of wood.

She spotted her before Elle could retreat and said, "I figured you might be back by now. With news."

Before Elle could answer, she added, "They never got far. Mr. Dean and the three others returned that same night." She waited for Elle to respond and when nothing came back, she continued. "Still and all, they are safe. And grateful. Like the captain you were with told us. Just got lucky, I suspect. House barely touched, even the lime grove mostly alright."

Elle knew she didn't think luck had anything to do with it. Just God's Will shining down on her squat, sullen boys, herself, and her beanpole husband. *Business as usual.*

She paused, aware of looking scuffed, her hair damp, and face red. Mrs. Dean must really want to know what happened, desperate for news on who was floating bum up in the silt. Elle imagined her pulled between two poles— disappointed that Elle was back but eager for the gossip. By now, Elle had raised herself up to fighting height. "Not everyone doing well as you are, but I suppose you already know that."

"Oh, yes. Terrible tragedy. Pastor plans to get to them as soon as he can."

"Might be too late for that, ma'am. Lots have fancy words for the men. In fact, that's all they seem to have. What they might need is a good meal and a warm, dry place to count their losses, and a promise that they won't have to fish their decaying buddies out of the drink, in return for pay of a tin of cold beans." Without being aware of it, Elle's voice had risen louder and louder. She wanted to tell the woman that maybe they should take a family in instead of all the empty talk, but was afraid of what else might come out once she got going.

A veil of fear passed across Mrs. Dean's face, causing Elle to still her tongue.

"I brought supplies," Mrs. Dean said nervously. "I know how careful the owners are about their provisions," she added, nodding and blinking at her boys.

The boys moved forward at her gesture, each holding something. Arthur, the bolder of the two, ran up to her and threw a green duffel at her feet. The younger kid held out the sack, never moving his eyes from the ground around her feet.

"Mighty kind of you and your kin," Elle said, resisting the impulse to refuse her offering. When she raised her eyes to meet Mrs. Dean's, she made out the merest shadow of pity. The bag landed at her feet.

"Careful when you open it. There's seeds in there. Seeds for you to grow more tomatoes, a hacksaw for Billy." Mrs. Dean grabbed ahold of her skirts, making her way toward Elle, eyes rubbering around the place to the small shack, then to Elle's disheveled bedding where she spent the night.

"Pastor sends regards. Asks if Billy needs anything, of course."

"Billy might not be coming back any time soon. They say the storm wiped out most of the old soldiers at the workcamp."

Mrs. Dean was silent then moved in awkwardly, taking Elle's hand between her palms and pressing it tightly. "Oh, Elle. I'm so sorry." And Elle could have sworn that she caught the smallest wave of sincerity in her voice for the only thing that Elle was happy to be rid of.

The women stood silent, until Elle broke the mood. "Went up but couldn't identify his body."

Mrs. Dean's hand shot up to her mouth and Elle almost laughed out loud.

"You better be able to find him. Leastways, if you want claim to this property. Without that and a proper marriage license, you won't be able to stay here."

"The place is mine. I paid for it."

"I thought Billy bought it."

"With what? His dollar a day from the government? Don't think he cared one whit about it."

"Not from what he told my husband. But still, good that you have the deed. If not, land'll revert back to the previous owner, or the government, within the year. I've seen it happen, especially around here, with everything so slapdash. Anyhow, you'll want to do him a proper Christian burial."

"No time for that now. Heard tell they're going to burn the bodies. Disease and all that." As she spoke, a small fear began to wend its way through her body. Did the shack belong to her? The land? She blinked the thought away, reached for the sacks and nodded. "Mighty thoughtful of the two of you. Send my thanks, if you would be so kind."

She nodded at the boys who had already turned away from her.

Even in death Billy wanted a hold of her future, mocking her actions, sending his minions to do the dirty to her.

As they moved toward their mother, the cat gave out a series of gasps and the boys turned back around.

Mrs. Dean asked, "That a puppy? A cat? Good on you. Leastways you'll have something to keep you company, something of your own to care for." She slapped Jimmy, the younger son, on the back of the head, turning him toward the path out before he got any ideas about looking to see what kind of animal she had. Mrs. Dean had gotten what she wanted. She would take these facts and stretch them out, giving herself plenty to spread around and mull over in the long, hot days ahead.

The cat's one good eye was closing but before he went back to sleep, she placed him on the ground. The outline of his ribs showed through easily, no fur at all on his stomach. Elle reached into the bag Mrs. Dean had left and pulled out a jar of fish in brine. She pried open the lid and the small cat half-sprinted, half-flopped up and at it, and she moved it away from him, feeling around in the bag to see if there were more. She felt at least a half-dozen jars and tins, so she took out a small piece of fish and placed it on a shard of coral and the cat was fast upon it.

As quick as he started, he began to convulse. It was the brine. Elle left him there, the memory of her poor poisoned dog returning with force. Convinced that the cat was dying, she moved away so she would not witness his desperation. Once she was far enough away, she tried to busy her mind by remembering that she needed to find the nice limestone well with its fresh water supply. The hermit had pointed it out to her and she had used it to wash and polish the fruits before selling them. If it was gone or somehow harmed by the storm, she would have little chance of prevailing. But she could not bear the sounds of the small animal suffering, so she returned and placed his heaving body in a shaded shelter, and poured the last of her warmed jug of water over him to cool him off before she left. *I've done all I can to help him.*

The marker she placed at the lip of the well would be long gone, blown and washed away. The landscape was altered, askew since the surge, but using the wharf as her guidepost, she moved to where she thought the hole had been. Almost instantly, she was up to her knees in water. Tricked by vegetation that only appeared anchored, Elle made out giant, silvered tree trunks and patches of thatch. A tin door surged gently in the water, rolling forward, then back out to reveal a sliver of blue that marked the water's rise. The storm had done more damage than she had first believed, fooling her into thinking she was safe.

She made out a sound that she thought belonged to a bird but, it was the cat, yelling from the side that she had supposed was her escape route. He seemed to be standing upright on solid ground, but it didn't follow that it would support her just because it held him. Still, she had no other clue to go by so she veered toward him, feeling first with her hands, then elbows, finally climbing on the boggy ground, knees first.

The cat began to walk away from her, his gait more stable, and she followed him to a mound of leaves and heard a low gurgling noise. He stopped to paw at the leaves, brushing them away. It was water. He had found a well, and she wanted to pick him up and squeeze him, but instead cupped some in her hands and began to drink, swirling the liquid around in her mouth; it tasted pure and sweet.

She closed her fingers tightly, cupping some and holding it out to the cat that now panted with heat. He almost passed out, and she cradled his head, pried open his sharp sawteeth, and used her finger as a spigot, guiding droplets of water into his mouth. He slowly began to swallow, finally gulping it down. When he stopped, she splashed some over his head, his eye, looking for infection, but it seemed to be closing, forming a tender scab. She cupped more water and bathed his bony body, making him look a little like a small brown bat. He was covered in sores from ticks and fleas, and she would wait to see if he got better before she doused him in enough kerosene to scare the vermin away. For now, they would both have to live with them.

Cat had shown her where the water was, so she knew she had to take care of him. Still, she feared the water hole was so close to the sea that it might not hold back the salt for long. There must be another source, but until she discovered it, this would have to do.

She felt hope rise up like an old, false friend, but refused to succumb to its trickery. The little cat, silently padding behind, followed her to the concrete foundation. Winds had blown the soggy edges of the island out to sea, pulling the rest closer to the shoreline.

Pastor was sure to come by soon asking her the "whys and wherefores" of Billy's disappearance. She needed to get an early start to the day and she had already spent most of the morning on the cat and the woman.

Colonies of tiny lizards and large beetles had already begun to burrow into the corners of her house now that it the floor was getting dry. She raked them out with an old broom stub she retrieved from under a pile of scrub. The bottom was still damp and she thought of what she might use for a makeshift roof. Maybe it wasn't so foolish to have gotten the sink first, she thought, imagining a costly roof sailing on the winds during the storm. She lay fronds over the hard floor then hollowed a spot, lining it with the oilcloth, where she would store food and dry goods, imagining every hungry critter silently watching, waiting for her to abandon her guard.

Laying in a stock of water in one of the buckets from the lodge, she opened the sacks from Mrs. Dean and made out a two or three week supply of food, if she were careful and caught some fish. She took out feed for the chicks and soon they were chirping and bobbing happily, the small cat in the center while they ran around him, up and over his body, oblivious to the danger. In case he got any ideas, Elle opened a bit of dried fish and swelled it with water for the orange cat, who she thought she would call One-Eyed Jack, maybe Cat for short.

Somehow she would find help, haul planks to make a ribcage for the roof. Thatch, she could weave herself, from what was lying about. She had seen it done and could find out the particulars easily enough. That was as far as she could dream for now, refusing to let her mind turn around too many corners. She had the seeds, the secret knowhow of growing them, and the beauty of this place that was now hers alone, free from fear of Billy.

25

Elle's mind raced. She knew she would have to pay a visit to the hermit and ask about the deed. He would know; maybe he would even help her. She had to fight her old habit of putting off all things unsavory. That inclination would do her in if she didn't take care of it. Maybe she should have promised the stupid woman that Billy was on his way back. Anything to keep her at bay.

Problem was she had never been to the hermit's shack, always met him at the grove, neither of them pleased to be together in tight quarters, if truth were told.

Although sightings of the hermit were rare, everyone wanted his fruit at harvest time. He had the touch, the secret of growing the tastiest sapodillies, alligator pears, and perfect tomatoes. He only relaxed when he spoke of his plants and trees. The only lecture he had ever given her was when he predicted that within ten years, sapodillies would be more common than oranges throughout Florida and the almighty United States. The great Florida growers got much of their knowledge from him way back when, and the only reason he was in No Name was the abundance of fresh water and his distaste of human company. He simply could not abide his fellow man.

Fruit trees had to be handled different here — simply too hot to follow traditional growers' practices. Many died off, the harvest barren from humidity and pests that feasted before man got his chance. When the fruit reached perfection, golden orbs formed, strong and heavy, ripening for a solid month, only to be stripped clean in a single night by some slithery interloper. If it wasn't that, it was the lack of water or, too much of it. And if someone managed to produce a bumper crop, then so did everyone else, most likely, and this drove prices down for everyone. Stories abounded of families trying to grow sun loving tomatoes, thinking it would be easy, but the sun was so intense and the air so salty that one or the other always proved their undoing.

Only the hermit did what no one else had been able to manage — he grew tomatoes in the shade of his fruit trees and fed them peculiar and exacting concoctions from the sea. When the hermit's crops went to market, they were burnished, crimson, and juicy.

In the early months, Elle, not knowing enough to be fearful of the old man, thought he was right amongst his own, saw him as one more strange critter on No Name, like the rattlers and scorpions. She saw no need to fear him as others did; he only got angry if he were crossed. Otherwise, all he asked was to be left alone. She offered help in his orchard and he took her up on it, leaving tools for her to work with on the edge of his land. She soon figured how much he disliked words, and that suited her just fine.

She quickly improved on his method of protecting tomatoes by scattering eggshells around their base. The hermit must've liked it well enough, leaving her to her own devices. She'd seen him no more than a few times in the seven months she lived there, usually at planting and harvest. It took little time to tend to the grove, so she did it between chores for No Name, gaining some food, a little money — made arrangements with small grocers and other straggler merchants who eked out a living with small deals — and a lot of know-how. The hermit seemed happy enough with the arrangement because it freed him from painful dealings with people. The longest conversation they had was when he first directed her to the abandoned cistern to store his fruit before the boat came to take it out. He asked her to move it there, and she offered to stay overnight, alone at the place, to guard against interlopers of whatever variety.

She would never have known this old cistern existed if he hadn't walked her there, pushing past a fence of trees and bush. Once inside, she spied a sign on a stick lying on the ground. He picked it up and jabbed the crudely painted sign into the ground with much cursing and jumping about. It read "Keep Out!" in black letters, a sloppy skull and crossbones done in faded red paint.

"This your storage place?" she had asked him and he nodded yes. Elle covered the crates of fruit with tarps and blankets and settled in for the night, hoping the boat would arrive at first light to take his produce to market. That night she slept peacefully in an ample hammock, under the magnificent sky, smudge pot burning in a vain effort to keep the bugs at bay.

Next morning, the boat came good and early, and Elle moved to the pier to greet the men. "Here representing the Russian," she said. For the life of her, she could never manage to pronounce his name.

"You talking about the hermit?"

She nodded yes, and the thin, old man, his long, grey hair tucked under a dirty white cap, handed her a packet with cash inside. When she reached for the envelope, a young and squat, bare-chested man in torn short pants moved to haul the crates onboard.

"Whoa. Hold yer horses. Got to count it first."

The old guy let out a breath, tapped his foot impatiently, and gave Elle a dirty look.

"Thought you wanted the tomatoes?" Elle said, barely glancing at him, intent on counting the cash.

"Paid for them. Included in the packet."

"You must take me for a fool. This paltry sum pays for the fruit only. Another Thirty-two for the tomatoes."

"Thirty-two dollars? Must be razzing me."

"No, sir. On the level. These here are prime. Take a looksee." Elle closed her eyes and felt around for a tomato in the crate, as if to prove that they were all perfect. "Take a bite out of this looker. Go on."

His eyes narrowed but he leaned forward to take it, holding it up close to inspect it.

Elle spoke again, pushing her advantage. "Can't get them anywhere south of the Carolinas. All have the blight but these." Elle wasn't sure it was true but had overheard it from one of the fisherman who stayed at the lodge from time to time. She had made him a big breakfast and he was surprised at the thick tomato slices on his plate and told her about the blight.

"Can't imagine what kind of fancy price you can resell them for, but no problem. If you don't want them, there's plenty that do. So go ahead and haul the fruit out but leave those back. That's the price, no discussion, less you have a problem with the fruit as well."

She turned to walk away, having no one else who would pay for the eight crates of tomatoes if he didn't buy them. Worse, he might abandon the fruit as well.

"Maybe I'll just buy the tomatoes, leave the sapodillies behind."

"Package deal. Got to take 'em all. Got no time to waste, and like I say, plenty more interested if you ain't. So what's it to be, cause I got to be off."

"Give you twenty dollars."

They finally settled on $25.00, and it was pure profit, almost a month of Billy's wages. Elle took the cash and pondered what to do with it. But fearful that word would reach him, she decided to tell the hermit.

Elle felt peaceful inside that small space, and soon she had another idea. Maybe the hermit would trade her work for this place and, in time, she might have something of her own, and enough space to start her own crops.

Within the week, she wrangled the deed from the crazy old man, along with a promise to sell the fruit from here, same as always. Just like Billy to find out the moment when she stood to gain. Not two months later, he had sold her out, the deed in pieces. But no use thinking on the past, better to find a way to fix it.

26

Over the better part of the late afternoon, Elle created a makeshift pulley system, struggling with an oversized oilcloth tarp, finally stretching it into position to create half a roof. With the place swept out, the table set off the ground on rocks, oilcloth overhead, she surveyed the cistern she planned to call home and brought out her kerosene lamp. She sat cross-legged at the salvaged door she would use as an eating table, and laid out the fare—the cans and jars, the twine rope and knives. But she could not enjoy the order she had muscled from mayhem nor take refuge in the past. Squinting into the kerosene light, she knew that she had two more chores before the day's end.

Again, Elle looked to the copse that held Billy's carcass. She imagined ravenous crabs working their way through Billy's grim flesh. Only five days since the storm and lots to get through. Guests never visited No Name this time of year and if they came, she would see them before they saw her. Even if they somehow got ahold of the traps, all they would see would be crabs going at each other. Unless they found the duffle and gunny sack that held his head and torso. Elle had no taste for fishing out Billy's remains, and within minutes had convinced herself to put it off for one more day, bargaining with herself that she would do a better job in the early morning light. That left just one more thing before nightfall.

With Cat tucked in and the chicks full and tired, she took off down the pathway opposite the lodge and into the brush that the hermit certainly owned. Although fallen trees and roots marred the way, ruts in the road read like signs telling the tale of her secret place. She noticed things she would normally have no use for, and made mental notes to gather them for her new home. Down the darkening pathway, memories came unbidden of the man who looked at her like he was staring down a rat hole.

Elle stopped for a bit and sat on a stump to think, not sure if she had gone too far in. Trees loomed overhead, one holding an air plant that tumbled at her feet, making her jump. It looked like the severed head of a castaway. She spun around, senses sharp, listening, sniffing the air. Great murky pools couldn't be avoided as she made her way deep into the brush, remembering when she had first seen this place. The few families that settled on No Name always started off strong. Monty had warned her about what hard living in the Florida Keys could do to a body. The women tried hard not to hate it when they first arrived, young and determined, hanging on to some man's vision, till they got older. People eventually knew them by their yellowed teeth, their necks scrubby like fighting chickens, mouths clamped tight, hands with flesh that quickly loosed from bone.

A hawk circled overhead, startled by her movement, and she almost walked past the tree that now resembled a grey tangle of thorns. Elle did not quite recognize what she was seeing. On the ground was a rubber arm with stitching as if to hold a sleeve no longer there. A child's lost toy, sun darkened, like livid flesh. It was a sign, lying inside the thorny tangle of the manchineel tree. She wrapped cloth around a branch of the tree and hacked it off with her knife. Somehow she was not surprised that the tree had withstood the storm perfectly intact.

When she returned to her small house, she covered the branch in cloth and buried it in a shallow grave. This talisman against harm complete, she decided she would wait until morning to deal with the body in the roots. By early darkness, she had mercifully fallen into a sleep so dense that it lasted the entire night.

27

She awoke from a dream of Billy whispering to the pastor, terrified that it was real. She had always avoided pastor's gaze because he looked at her as if she was something pitiable that lived underwater. *Never know what Billy said about me.* Billy had never been much on planning, but when he wanted, he worked like five of her on the roads or at the lodge. And now she understood why—he had to. It was simple as that. She discovered the secret to growing things in this impossible soil. When she set to planting the seeds on the bed of eggshells, next to the others, he would not admit that she had a gift, and instead of being happy that he had a capable wife, he hated her for being able to coax bounty out of rock bed. He never understood that he would benefit most.

As the day wore on, again Elle didn't make it to the crab traps, paralyzed by an unreasoning fear of what was waiting for her. She lined up jars of food and put them away, then lined them up again, counting them over again. Everything was running low and no ferry had come for days.

Over the next few days, her resolve always disappeared

by late morning. Elle dawdled, waiting for the gumption to go back to Billy's resting place, pull up a couple of traps to see what remained of the body.

Relief that no one had appeared on the horizon turned into worry as Elle waited on word from the owners, the iceman, and news of the ferry schedule.

The worst task — taking the duffle out into open water and sinking the head — became the thing she refused to think about. But the more she avoided it, the antsier she became. The dark of night, once a welcome end to her long workday, a time to reflect and relax, had turned into a time to fear. Her little homestead seemed shadowed by the lodge and the twisted mangrove island, its treetops visible from every angle.

She played with One-eyed Jack, cleaned the cistern properly, and managed to set up the sink, attaching it to a water barrel she had salvaged and stored in the icehouse before the storm hit. No matter how much she would have enjoyed this in times past, she now felt a prisoner of the place. She didn't like the thought of Billy so close that he could be spying on her while she labored.

Although she knew he had to be rousted, she couldn't grab hold of her anger for long enough to do the job. It moved just beyond her reach, turning itself inside-out into a mix of nerves and fear. But this place would never be hers so long as he remained at the bottom, beyond her reach, yet close enough to bob up any minute, most likely when someone was about. Billy had an uncanny knack of turning up at the exact wrong time.

Elle knew she had to rid the place of Billy's energy, set his spirit free from the traps, and sever his hold on her.

Finally, on the fourth day back, she was ready.

Everything was favorable. The water was calm, the sky cloudless. She woke up, Cat by her side, and began their ritual of stretching his back leg, forcing him to use it so the muscle wouldn't stiffen. He fought her at first, but then learned to tolerate it. She collected her lightest clothing from the drying rock, walked to the pier, untied her small rowboat, and stepped onboard.

Don't think. Don't think too hard on it. Just get it done. Her leg had mostly healed but for the thick, gnarled scar that settled on the length of her thigh. It only hurt when she knelt for long periods.

Cat followed her into the boat and she scuttled the two of them into the tangle, grateful she could chatter at him to keep up her nerve.

Outside the grove, chains holding the traps were clearly visible amongst the huddle of trees. The closer she got, the more she rushed. *What was I thinking, four days back? Why have I allowed so much time to go by?*

Lucky for her there were no guests snooping about. Elle was horrified as she neared the place. Anyone could make out the explosion of light when the sun hit the metal. And how tourists love the notion of pirate treasure out here. Maybe they would think they had seen the dazzle of coins, hidden riches.

A large, silver chain had blackened in the water, and Elle recognized it as the one that hooked the duffel. With one foot on a protruding root, she braced herself by placing the other on a sturdy branch, unhooked the chain from the "v" in the tree trunk, and wrapped it around her wrist a few times. Using both hands, she tugged to get the measure of the thing and was pleased to feel it lift. She pulled steady, and the heavy duffel rose, water streaming out from all sides.

Elle did not want to touch it and wondered if she might be able to swing it onto the boat, but thought better of it and took it by the handles, laying it gently in the boat, dreading to hear the thud, her imagination jumping.

She half expected to see a boat pull in, such was Billy's devilish luck. But no, no boats were in sight, the sky was still blue, dark water lapped gently, birds flew overhead.

Elle cranked the engine and spoke into the air, Cat purring, enjoying the attention. The small skiff moved steadily through the twisted channels and sharp turns, and still Elle talked out loud, causing Cat to chirp answers back at her, his voice anxious, his gaze questioning. On she sailed, past Grassy Key, the shore growing more ragged the farther she went. She passed a grim-faced reconnaissance crew, with a dive flag up, and knew she must travel farther up the Keys. The heat of the sun hit the duffel, the original green color drained to gray. A rank and ripe odor rose from the bottom of the boat and hung in the sodden air above them.

Elle cruised past Indian Key, and there she stopped the boat. She knew she had to untie the bag because if it was ever found, there'd be no explaining how it got there. Even the great storm couldn't manage to chop a head off, blow it into a duffel bag, and tie it up proper. Besides, it would decay faster it if wasn't protected.

Elle cut the small engine and struggled with the duffel, finally splitting it open along a rotted seam. The old habit of crossing herself came to her unbidden, but she resisted the impulse. Enough lies had happened.

When she opened the bag and turned it upside down over water, the head would not release. Hair was stuck in the lacing so she took the oar and tried to pry it out, but that didn't work. She almost lost enough control to toss the whole thing out, but finally, with tears streaming and some cursing, she stuck her hand in, grabbed a handful of hair that came off in her hand. She finally pulled his head out, turning away until the last minute before she looked at it. Relieved, she could see that Billy's spirit was gone, this ball of wax had nothing more to do with him. She tossed the head into the ocean, traveled another five or six miles before she sunk the duffel in water near a small island in the Middle Keys.

28

Although Elle tried to gun the engine to get back to No Name, it didn't have much juice left, so the trip took longer than she would have liked. She paddled a short distance and then remembered the old Conch's store in Grassy Key. Maybe she could distract herself by getting some goods for her home. The thought of good feed for the chickens and a bit of meat for Cat cheered her on, giving her purpose. Chances were if anyone in the Keys had groceries and supplies in stock, Q would. Please let it be there intact and not another victim of the storm.

She spotted it from the shore, its fool shade of bright pink caught in the sun. Maybe he wasn't so stupid after all. Everyone seemed to know him by the unnatural color of his establishment.

Rumor had it he could get almost anything. No one knew his proper name, all just called him Q. His business took off during prohibition, but he still kept good homemade stock around and always had high-grade rum from Cuba. He was a strange little guy, mostly kept to the business at hand, not big on words, which suited Elle just fine. He would have feed for the hens and maybe end pieces of meat or entrails for Cat. If she were lucky, she could find a cheap tarp so the owners would know she wasn't pilfering anything of theirs if they came upon her using it.

The store was nothing more than a concrete box, painted a bilious shade of pink, sitting on concrete blocks. Not much on the shelves, but Elle knew to ask for what she wanted and he would disappear somewhere out back, returning with the items in his arms. Where he put all that stuff in his tiny house had long been the subject of local speculation. Not seeing any oilcloth on the shelves, Elle asked for it, and Q raced out back, coming back in with a selection of three. She chose the cheapest, a bag of chicken feed, and a small slab of what he called beef.

"One dollar and forty cents, miss."

"I ain't buying no grocery order. Besides, the meat is barely this side of spoiled."

"Things dear these days. Scarce."

"Guess that's my answer, in which case we have no more business." Elle folded her five dollar bill back into her neck pouch and tucked it into her shirt.

As she turned to exit the store, she smelled something weedy burning, wafting in from a back room. A lanky kid opened the door and a woodsy puff of smoke lolled in the air behind him. Elle turned to where the smell came from.

"Sweetgrass is all," Q said, his face jutting toward her, daring her to comment. "We was about to close, which I think is a right good idea."

"I smell something else." Elle sniffed the air.

"How about a strong whiff of 'mind-your-own-business'? That's what else."

"You smudging? That sage?" Elle had heard of the

cleansing ritual the old Conchs used to rid the house of evil spirits. "You sell that stuff?"

"Who wants to know?"

"That sweetgrass from around these parts?"

"Yas'm."

"Got some to spare? Not askin' for no handout. I'll give you good money for it." She reached in her pouch as if to underline the offer.

"Can't sell it; won't do you no good if money changes hands for it. Drains it of all power. Has to be offered, free and easy."

Elle had heard of the powerful smudge made by the natives. Florida sweetgrass was known to be the best in the land. She had heard tell from some Conchs who came to do the boats. They swore by it.

"Where'd you get the sage?"

"Not your lookout. Time to close now, so fuel up, pay up, and be off with you." He folded his short arms tightly against his scrawny chest to underscore his words.

"Wait just one minute. Forgot to get those supplies I had on the counter. Don't know what I was thinking, putting them away." Elle tried to smile.

"Must be nerves," Q said, lifting his eyebrows slightly and looking at her dead on for the first time since she entered his store.

"Mighty anxious these days, what with all the trouble," Elle said, a cadaverous smile on her face.

Elle gathered up the tarp and the chickenfeed but left the small slab of what looked like beef in the makeshift cooler, a shard of ice all but melted.

The big-eared, wizened face of the Conch stared up at her. "Fergit summit?"

She sighed, but made no move to go get the supposed beef.

"Cause iff'n you do," Q said, "I might be tempted to forgit summit myself."

"How do I know it works?" Elle asked, returning with the small slab of meat and placing it on the stained wooden counter.

"Only three places left standing on all of Grassy Key after the storm. All you gotta know."

Elle left with her bundle, two dollars lighter, but three large smudge sticks to the good.

Maybe that old Conch was right and trying to make sense of the world was a slippery slope. Maybe there was something to the sticks.

By the time she docked at No Name, nightfall was closing in and it was too late to do the lodge proper. She made a fire on the piece of flat coral and found a second smooth door washed in from the storm that was bound to be useful for something. Jack the Cat was on the meat before she could cook it proper. She and Cat both limped, but only when they were tired. She tossed another piece of meat to where he wouldn't disturb the chicks that were scrambling to get at the feed.

Elle delayed going back to the lodge for the tent long enough for night to set in. No way she was going near the place in the dark. Soon the sun was shot down in the sky, and with the chickens clucking and Jack blinking at her from his perch in the tree with his one good eye, she clutched the sticks that she hoped would finally rid her of Billy and save the lodge from becoming a corridor for sorrowful shades to wander.

Tomorrow, she thought, just before she slept. Tomorrow she would make it right.

29

Next day Elle hauled herself up top of the dry cement wall and looked out to the water. The pier was bereft, waiting lonely and abandoned, Elle's ramshackle skiff tied haphazardly, more an insult to the ritzy pier than anything else.

Cat was on the ledge of the cistern, scratching idly at his caked-over eyehole, hoping for more beef.

Owners should be back soon, workmen too. But before Elle could bring herself to walk to the lodge, she eyed the small parcel of seeds that Mrs. Dean left her. She jumped from the ledge onto a large rock that broke the distance, Cat beating her to the ground.

Inside the bag, tomato seeds were neatly dried into a piece of muslin. Just seeing them gave Elle a surge of hope, as if preparing for the future was a charm against another deluge, Elle gathered up what passed for soil, formed it into a pile, and set it atop the shiny oilcloth in open air, letting the sun have at it, to bake and burn away every nasty thing.

She planned to mound it up into a couple dozen small piles, stick a seed in each, placing each in a pouch to make them easy to water. The weather was perfect for starting things. It didn't make any difference to her that she wouldn't get much money for the tomatoes. Starting up again was all that mattered.

In three short months, Elle would have a grove of bright red tomatoes bursting with seeds, the large field fenced in by sapodillies and lime trees. She would be awash in seeds, maybe sell those as well, start a mail-order business. They fetch a good and dear price up north. Tomatoes would pay for the rest of the grove, and her job as first cook would keep her and the critters until everything came into bearing.

Elle refused to think beyond that, only allowing herself to daydream about the house with a stove and a horsehair mattress, a good chair or two, and a pantry stocked with supplies. No men—not ever again—although her mind began to bend in that direction before she took hold of it. "Don't never learn, do ya?" she said out loud, images of Jim lying beneath her, the boat rocking, the two of them coming unbidden.

Once into the clearing, an insistent, dull banging seemed to follow her, causing Elle to turn and investigate. A couple of crab traps had returned to shore and were slapping against the wharf, and Elle had to look. The lodge had lost two or three dozen of them to the storm. Chances were they would be empty. What were the odds of Billy coming loose? Seemed to Elle that every time she ventured toward the lodge, something happened that stopped her in her tracks. Still and all, she must see for herself. She steeled her shoulders and turned, walking to water's edge. Mouth set, knuckles white, Elle peered in to find nothing there. She gathered up the loose traps, spied a few more bobbing further out, caught in trees on the other side of the pier, and vowed to get those as soon as she prepared the lodge.

The walk down the pathway was muddy, and her shoes kept getting sucked into puddles, the ground strewn with stuff she hadn't seen the day before. The aftermath of the storm spit up everything from lumber to lace hankies—a fool's paradise for beachcombers.

She spotted a large, golden feather with a black tip and picked it up, wiping the mud onto her pants. *This will do nicely. Just like the Conch told me—has to be a found feather.* Elle clutched the feather then patted the outline of the two smudge sticks in her pouch, having left the third behind against another mishap. *First, do the lodge, then myself, then the crab traps.*

After gathering the hodgepodge of tarpaper, tools and oddments scattered willy-nilly around the building, Elle made neat piles of the rest of the debris, stacking the traps by the icehouse, calmed and cheered by the renewed orderliness.

Elle felt the impression of matches in the pouch around her neck, all the while deeply breathing in the odor of the sage and sweetgrass sticks, as if to dispel spirits by exhaling on them. *If this is the silliest thing ever, how come I feel jittery again, so filled with spirit? Here goes nothin'.*

The door creaked open and an overwhelming odor of damp and something else hit her when she entered. The light was dim but Elle did not reach for a lamp. She knew where she had to go. She pulled out a smudge stick and lit a match on the wall, something she would ordinarily have no truck with. The stick flamed when she first lit it, and she stuck it in her mouth and puffed on it to make sure it continued to burn. The acrid taste was not unpleasant, and it fogged her mind almost instantly. In the blue afternoon light, she held the smudge stick in one hand and the feather in the other hand, wafted the smoke toward her heart, then her head, then the rest of her body. Before she could get the incantation out, she saw something, like a shadow, move to the spot where she had dealt Billy the initial blow. It disappeared as soon as she saw it but then reappeared on the wall in the form of a dark red outline of his crumpled body. Elle's chest tightened, and she felt a sharp, slicing pain in her thigh, exactly where Billy had struck her. Instead of catching her breath, she took a long, deep draught of smoke and extended her arms over the exact spot where the bed had been. She closed her eyes tightly and moved the stick around, invoking her wishes, first in a low growl, then gathering in strength, growing louder:

Begone, Billy Woodman.
And haunt me no more.
Let this blessing and smoke
kick you on out the door.

She moved around mechanically, wafting smoke from the smudge stick into every corner of the room after setting her intention and smudging herself as protection against evil spirits. From time to time, she took a large puff against the stick going out. She said it again, this time venting her anger:

Begone, Billy Woodman.
And haunt me no more.
Let this blessing and smoke kick your sorry behind
Out the goddamned door.

She returned to the center of the room and tried to remember exactly what the old Conch had told her — something about looking up towards the heavens, first sending smoke skyward, then to the floor. She took a few more puffs on the stick to help her remember. By the time she entered the great room, she found the procedure hilariously funny and had forgotten many of the words. She stood in the doorway, scratching her head, inhaling deeply when she heard something groan. She opened the door to her old bedroom with the blue posy wallpaper, but the sound was coming from the front of the lodge. She stood smack center of the doorway between the hall and the room when the front door to the lodge snapped open.

The dark, smoke-filled hallway made it impossible to see anything and Elle, gripped with fear, could not call out. She heard footsteps on carpet and pushed herself through, back into the bedroom, onto the small bed, staring wide-eyed into the doorway.

There were at least two of them. She heard whispers, but neither sounded like a man. The owners. Please be the owners come to have a looksee at the place. It would be natural, Elle thought, trying to convince herself it was so.

She dropped the remains of the stick, but quickly picked it up and took another deep puff before crossing it around her body for luck. Then she snuffed the stub out between her thumb and forefinger, put it into her pouch, and tucked that inside her shirt.

She heard shuffling, then coughing. With great relief, Elle realized she had never heard of demons having a coughing fit then reminded herself that she didn't believe in demons. For some reason, her imagination was having a heyday with her. She felt angry and sad and giddy, all at the same time. And then she recognized a voice. It was Monty from the ferry. She hadn't seen or heard word from him since the day of the storm, when he left with the guests of No Name.

"Monty," she shrieked, jumping up off the bed, happy to hear his voice. Elle rushed out of the room, tears streaming from her eyes. Two clouds of smoke collided, battling it out in the doorway.

"Lord have mercy." Mrs. Dean stared at her, "It's the cook. Her again."

"Elle..." Monty seemed more surprised than happy to see her. "What the dilly-o? What you been doin' here?" He nodded and widened his eyes in warning as if to caution her that Mrs. Dean was present, but it made no sense to Elle. Anyhow, what Elle did was none of her concern.

"Smudging, and I don't care who knows it. Owners won't mind. Might even be grateful if it comes to that." Elle thought quickly, her mind clearing. "The storm and all, and this being No Name, in the middle of the kingdom of the almighty Conch." Elle found this funny and to her surprise, even Mrs. Dean seemed to be holding back the giggles.

"Not right," Mrs. Dean said and made the sign of the cross herself, but her heart didn't seem to be in it. "Can't breathe," she said as she turned back, banged into a wall then headed out the front door.

Monty turned to Elle. "Smudging, huh?" he said and winked at her. "Been to see Q, the old Conch at Grassy Key, I can tell. Used to be in the booze business back when." He winked again. "I come to check on the place then bring a small party in."

"Someone fool enough to want stay here? Right after the storm? And in September, with the heat, and it being high bug season? Don't make sense," Elle said.

"Sorry. Couldn't warn you, but the place always looks good and they can leave any time they want. Got a big boat at the ready. You know how some have the fishin' fever."

"Awright. Must be very important people for the owners to open it up just for them. Maybe close friends of the owner? Anyhow, it makes no never-mind to me. They pay me the same to be here, no matter."

"Got their own cabin. Guess they want to check on it. But you got to make up the cabin that rents by the week. Anyhow, I also had to bring Mrs. Dean back to No Name." Monty took his hat off as if he suddenly realized something important. "Oh, Elle. Is Billy still here? Good on him that he didn't make the last run up to Matecumbe. Always had the luck of the devil, that guy."

Elle remembered the morning before the storm hit, Monty motioning for her to get aboard, and the mayhem of people trying to make it out on the last ferry. "But he did get on the ferry," she said. "Haven't seen hide nor hair of him since."

"No, certain he did not," Monty said.

"You know what he was like. Never paying. Always hiding in cars." Before Monty could argue the point, Elle said, "Saw him get on myself, maybe you wasn't paying proper attention. He always was a sneaky one."

Monty shrugged. "Not going to argue. Believe whatever you like. Now I got to get a move on."

Elle followed Monty outside the lodge, where he nearly tripped over Mrs. Dean, who was standing close to the doorway where she had likely heard every word.

Monty nodded in Mrs. Dean's direction. "She and Pastor been offering comfort at the church and at the school. Good people."

When he disappeared behind the lodge, Elle opened and shut the front door like a giant fan to force the smoke out. Wind began to blow from out of nowhere, as it is wont to do in these parts, picking up in speed, followed by the sky darkening.

She was trapped by Mrs. Dean, something she dreaded. She wanted to follow Monty, but the woman grabbed ahold of both her hands, and peered intently into her face, looking for an opening into her sorrows. Elle lowered her eyes, more from wanting to escape than feelings of contrition.

"It's alright, dear," the woman said. "You most certainly do not have to say anything to me. In time, it will all come out. A light will shine on a pathway and show you how to lift up your burden."

Elle knew she was desperate to learn more about Billy's fate. She wanted to witness Elle's horror and loss, even if only secondhand.

"The old soldiers paid the price, Mrs. Woodman, and I suppose they are looking down on us right now. But it is not for us to question why some escaped, and others perished."

Elle envisioned rich vacationers driving off the ferry in their fancy cars and getting the dickens out of the storm's pathway. The soldiers had no such option.

Mrs. Dean patted Elle's hands. "Pastor Dean sends his blessings. And some tools for Billy, if he turns up."

"Billy won't be needing no tools, Mrs. Dean."

The woman let out breath and Elle took the opportunity to snatch her hands away.

"He's with the others, stacked up like cordwood in Islamorada."

"I thought they weren't sure..." Mrs. Dean looked horrified.

"He's what?!"

It was a woman's voice, one Elle instantly recognized though she had only suffered a single conversation with her.

Elle had been so wrapped up in Mrs. Dean's stare that she hadn't seen or heard Monty return. He was back with three strangers and Billy's strumpet with the red lipstick, Mrs. Rowlands. The woman repeated herself, "He's what? What did you say?"

Mrs. Rowlands wore another absurd white dress, this one with little brown sprays on it that made it look like someone had spit on her. It had about the same heft as the frilly curtains, the sleeves and flouncy neckline doing a jig whenever the slightest breeze hit. The other couple looked around with a slightly incredulous expression on their faces, as if they couldn't quite figure what this place was all about.

"I asked you something, missy." Mrs. Rowlands was staring at her, her head jutting out like a chicken, her lips in a curl.

It sounded more like a statement than a question to Elle. Elle felt a thrill of fear course through her body.

The pastor's wife explained, "Taken by the storm with the others. That's what must have happened to poor Billy."

It took a moment for Elle to realize what was happening. The pastor's wife continued speaking, addressing the entire group, "This Sunday we are having a special service. Just a little country place, but the Lord visits us there, just the same. We'd be honored to have you all as guests. Pastor's got a fitting sermon, what with all the sorrowful events." She saved the tail end of her smile for Elle then she strode off, pausing when she reached the corner to raise her hand in a combination wave and benediction.

Monty spoke. "Dan coming in later, maybe as late as tomorrow, to set up the boat for fishin'. Heard tell that kingly feasts follow storms. Strange fish and stunned sea creatures come in for the taking."

"Meanwhile," said Elle, "I got to set up the guest

cottage. Last person what stayed there forgot to close the window and the mattress got spoilt with rain and such. So don't know where to put you all."

Mr. Rowlands had on a seersucker suit, his white bowtie loosed on account of the heat. His trousers were wrinkled, the hems soaked halfway up to the knee. His hair was an unnatural dull black. Looks like shoe polish, Elle thought, and when she looked closer, she saw a dark bead of sweat wend its way down the planes of his face and disappear into a deep, jowly wrinkle. That poor so and so. No doubt about it. He's fixin' color in his hair.

"Don't suppose there's any grub to be had?" he asked, placing a possessive arm around Mrs. Rowlands. "Maybe all you ladies ought to whip something up for us?" He winked at Mrs. Rowlands, who made what she must have thought was a cutesy bunny face back at him.

She still looks the trollop, Elle thought, and walked back toward the lodge, pleased that she didn't have to answer the woman. "I'll get the key for your guests, sir, cabin number 18. Just changed the mattress for mine. Almost new, though."

Elle patted the few dollars she had in her pouch, taking a weird satisfaction in knowing they were from the Rowlands woman. She gets 'em from him and me from her, she thought, suddenly regretting that she had lost any to the fire.

"Number 18?" Monty spoke. "I stayed there last time I were here. I'm sure I locked that window up tight." Elle felt bad for Monty, who was meticulous about closing up neatly, so as not to wear out his welcome at No Name Lodge.

The six of them stood awkwardly in a loose circle, the Rowlands woman looking through her own husband, now with a second stream of black dye bleeding into his collar. *Why doesn't she help him? At least take the handkerchief from his pocket and hand it to him.*

Elle said, "And who will I be preparing dinner for? I don't believe I have gotten your names. Sir?"

Monty spoke, "These are the Newman's, Mr. and Mrs." Monty looked from the group to Elle and said, "This here's Elle, best little cook this side of Miami."

"Okay, okay," Mr. Rowlands said, dismissing Monty with an imperial wave of his hands, his large, ruby-embedded gold signet ring catching the light. "Now let's get moving. I need to get away from these bugs." He turned to his wife. "You got the key, darling?"

While Mrs. Rowlands fussed with her purse, Elle went into the lodge, returning with the key to cabin 18, along with four silk paper fans, a sheet of instructions, and a shopping bag with jigsaw puzzles and board games.

"Dinner is no more'n a couple of hours away. Meantime, I'll bring a plate of sandwiches around."

"Drinks, too," Mr. Newman said, swatting at flies and looking up at the heavens as if wondering what else they would have to endure.

30

Once they were out of sight, Monty turned as if to go back to the boat.

"No way, mister." Elle said.

"What?"

"Don't think you're goin' anywhere and leaving me with the likes of them. What was you plannin' on? I need me some help with them."

"You've handled much more than four people and I got the fisherman on the way. They just want you to do the cooking and cleaning. What's your deal, Elle?"

"Precious little ice, no fresh meat, and I don't like the woman. How's that for starters?"

"Which woman? Mrs. Dean won't be back, Elle, and anyhow, you ought to take it easy on her."

"Not her, it's the Rowlands woman."

Elle wondered how much she should tell Monty and what he suspected. She was fearful of returning to the lodge and wanted him with her.

"You don't look good," Monty said. "Got too much on your mind. We been through a lot, too. Had to tough it out in the water car in the storm." Monty appeared weather-beaten, now that she noticed.

"Never thought to ask. Oh, Monty. So sorry."

"Naught to be sorry for. We're the lucky ones, for sure." Elle noticed that Monty kept his hat on. When she looked closely, she saw the edge of a bandage above his right ear. She pointed to it. "Bad for business," he said, "so I keep the hat on. Healing up nicely, thanks for asking."

"Stay while I make up the sandwiches. Then you can go. Feeling a little of the heebie-jeebies, is all."

"Aftermath of the sticks, leaves you feelin' like all the world is talking behind your back." He winked at her.

Elle stared at the door, willing her body to enter the lodge. As she stared at it,

Monty spoke. "What happened to the bed, Elle? Everything right as rain when we left."

Darn it all. This lodge will be my undoing.

"No worries, mister. I dragged mine to your cabin. Don't ask. Maybe your guest?" Elle tried to make her voice sound light, make a joke of it, but Monty was having none of it.

"You mean that singer? Oh no, she had nothing to do with anything. No more'n five foot, if she's an inch. Couldn't reach the window, wouldn't know how to use them window levers. Besides, I made sure to close the windows tight before I left."

"I haven't said word one to the owners. I'll just get another mattress for my room. Leave it to me." Elle hated to blame Monty, but he had no real stake in the place.

Elle didn't hear his reply; she had begun to ponder Mrs. Rowlands's visit. Just when she was getting a foothold on the place, that strumpet shows up to snoop around. Could she be that smitten, or was she just mean, wanting what was never hers, and for all of four hundred dollars? It may seem a lot of money when you have none, but even Elle knew it was a pittance, payment for an abandoned cistern on a half-acre of shifting rockbed.

Elle dug her nails into her palms and Monty stood there under the thundering sky, eyeing her strangely.

They went into the lodge and lit lamps, the smoke now stale. Elle stepped into the large walk-in pantry, pondering the selection of tinned goods. She started up the fire in the stove and looked for dry yeast to start making dough to rise. Meantime, she found crackers, some sprats and pickles, and a couple packages of small tea cakes. The icehouse hadn't been tended to since the storm, so there was no fresh food or produce to be had.

Darn them anyhow. It's as much trouble to open the place for the four of them as it would be for a crowd and, a whole boatload more nerve wracking. And now she was alone here steppin' and fetchin' and seeing to their every little need. More than one thing just wasn't right. The men didn't seem to be too keen on fishing from what she saw. Looked to Elle like that Rowlands woman was running the show. She had brought them here, Elle was pretty sure. *But why?*

Elle stared at the floorboards, thinking, always thinking. It was a curse. Monty came over and took her by the shoulders. Things had been so haywire that Elle wouldn't have been surprised if he tried to kiss her. He seemed to be aware of what she was thinking because he looked in her eyes, took his hat off, and smiled. Elle reached out, felt the bandage and saw the shaved head underneath.

"Will you get a load of us? What a pair we make," he said. "You with your wonky hand touchin' my head full of bandages."

"And not the only ones, Monty. Many in far worse shape'n us."

"Ain't that the truth."

She turned away from him but he touched her chin and said, "No worries, Elle. It's not like that. You're far too much of a thinking gal for my taste."

"Thanks be for that," she replied, smiling. "Sorry I can't say the same bout you."

They laughed, low smoke snaking in a shaft of light, and Elle had a sudden urge to confess, to confide exactly what had happened and why, but held her counsel.

Monty spoke, "You just gotta hang on here for a bit, Elle. Hang on like the devil to this job, this place. Many more womenfolk alone now, looking for whatever they can find to get by. If you thought work was scarce before this mess, just wait and see what happens now. Fool dunces running the show."

"You mean the government?"

"Didn't get the train out to the veterans on time. Didn't care enough to see to it. Plain and simple from where I sit. Lord knows how many widows and children left bereft."

"What about you, Monty? You still gonna run those rigs?"

"Government takin' over from the company. Same ferries with a fresh coat of paint and new names. Gonna run those same, like before. Government don't have to make a profit, so they say the fare will be good and low. I already got a handle on my old job. You know I cannot be cast aside." He smiled rakishly at her, cocking his head to the side, causing a flap of the bandage to come loose. "I know how hard you got to work to stay away from me, girl. That goes double for everyone else. Even the government wants to keep me around."

Elle had always seen the charmer in Monty but never quite felt it, more enjoyed watching it for the sport of the thing and the way it broke up the day for her when he was around. He had always taken a shine to her but it was more of the brotherly variety, for the most part. Still and all, he reminded her that she was a woman and she liked that well enough. Therein lay the man's charm—the easygoing trap that he sprung, practicing on her when no one else was about. The man can't help himself; it's in his bones. Still and all, she liked watching him reel them in, so long as she didn't swim too close to his hook.

Monty was still speaking, "And Elle. Maybe it ain't right for me to say this, but, you are still a fine looking woman under that scowl you wear like widow's weeds. Not a terrible thing to be rid of Billy. More a lodestone than a help, and you know it."

That was the longest and kindest speech she had ever heard from Monty except when he was putting it to the tourists. But this time he meant it, and she watched him as he spoke, not paying too much mind to the particulars.

"You need to put a little meat on those bones," she said, sizing him up.

"What? What are you on about?"

"Just lookin' out for you. Lord knows someone ought to do it." The knees of his navy pants had taken on a life of their own and his loose shirt made his chest look puny.

"Take off those things and I'll wash them for you. May as well add them to the load." Elle was forming an idea, and she didn't think it would be too rough going to talk him into it. It struck her as good for everyone all around. Everyone except for old man Rowlands, but Elle had no sympathy for him. He had made his bargain.

No telling when Mrs. Rowlands would bring up the $400 she had given Billy for the shack. Surely the husband didn't know about it, or she would have laid claim to it the minute they stepped onto the hallowed ground of No Name. No, that woman had plenty of her own to hide, maybe more than Elle. Besides, she didn't know thing one about what really happened to Billy Woodman. The last image Elle had of the woman was just before the storm, directing a few men onto the last ferry, each weighted down with her cases and parcels, and Mrs. Rowlands looking around frantically, as if trying to find someone or something she had misplaced. Billy, most likely.

31

No one went out the next day. The four of them ordered refreshments and set up in the cabins, getting up to lord-only-knows what. The little place was their own private party and all Elle did was trot supplies in and out, booze mostly, and found movie magazines for the women. The men wanted to dine in the lodge and Elle had to beg fish from the kayacker, calling him from the pier when she spotted him, giving him a sum from the money the owners left for just such an occasion.

Elle prepared the evening meal and cranked up the Victrola in the library to create a cheerful atmosphere for the small party. Maybe she could get on the men's good side with food. She brought out toast points with creamed onion on matching tin trays with fish scenes on them and dragged out the heavy set of green leather footrests, one for each guest. The banker motioned for her to lift one of his swollen legs and place it on the stool. He looked worn out, but from what, Elle could only imagine. His feet were as small and probably soft as a girl's. But no matter what she did for them, Mrs. Rowlands's look let her know that she was not taken in. *Okay, then. I'll kill her with kindness,* Elle thought. *Maybe the others will turn on her.* The thought made Elle smile — the four of them in a melee, Mrs. Rowlands catching the worst of it. All the more funny when she caught the woman scowling at her.

Elle's old bedroom was directly across from the library and she caught Mrs. Rowlands's eye wander there on occasion, making her want to go in and take a looksee that all was cleaned up. But Elle knew that would be impossible. The trouble was, she could only bear to enter the horrors of the place when other people were around, which was always the worst possible time.

No one was interested in going out on the boat. But the Rowlandses' party paid that boat a princely sum to sit idle, and the two men who ran it were having none of her wishes for fresh catch to feed them all. When asked, they said they were "under strict orders to loaf. Paid handsomely to sit and take in the scenery."

Elle understood that people such as the Rowlandses found it important that everyone be at the ready to wait on them. The only thing they enjoyed more was making a show of wasting money or food or time. Hers, mostly. It seemed to Elle that she was the only one doing any work, and she had little to show for it all.

She was having a time of it, going through the supplies in the cupboard, because the crazy man who filled up the icehouse was nowhere to be found. Elle suspected that the storm destroyed the machines and even the man who empties the slops probably skedaddled to parts unknown. Why did the owners agree to have this group here? It made no sense, what with all in disarray.

Elle thought hard about what she could do to please her

spoiled charges, always fearing that one false move could place her job in peril. She had to feed them well because that would be the first thing owners would ask; she had heard it a million times before. In fact, conversations generally started with the owners smiling and sniveling, asking, "And how did you find the food?" Boss would ask almost everybody this question, then stand back, ready for compliments to shower upon his oversized head as if he had made it with his own clumsy hands.

The last thing Elle wanted was to waste one of the few good hams on them, but she had to make a show of it. Maybe she could use the rest for sandwiches. But she had no ice to keep the leftovers fresh and couldn't imagine them having it a second day. It was hard to concentrate on food. She was always wondering if one of the crab pots had come up and if Billy was somehow making his way to the lodge. Then her mind wandered back to kitchen concerns, thinking about the ham again, imagining how much leftovers it would create. The more she thought, the crazier it seemed to cut into the ham.

No, she would use one of the cans of corned beef and make some of that strange asparagus vegetable in fancy aspic. If she used a little more of the Knox gelatin, she was sure it would set without having to be in the icebox. She got fresh eggs out, began work on a chess pie, and left the ham hanging in the larder. Would do her no good whatsoever for word to get around that No Name was anything less than hospitable.

Elle dipped her hands in flour and set about making dumplings to rise, although she had no butter to dress them up with. Drippings would have to do. Elle laughed when she thought of others being so impressed at what she came up with. "And she does all that fancy cooking without electricity," she said out loud in the kitchen, mimicking the showy warbler who took a shine to Monty, when she was talking to one of the guests. Truth be told, Elle wouldn't be able to make sense of a kitchen that actually had electricity, but let them think what they liked. Not her concern.

Here I am, she thought, *working in the lodge like nothing happened, forgetting about all the sorrows. I just bought me an hour off and it being not even a week into the loss of Billy. Maybe it's the smudge sticks, but it sure is good to forget about the traps, if only for a piece of the afternoon.*

Every day the thought of the traps came unbidden, as if in a wave. On the second day they were here, her four guests began to explore, starting with a walk out on the large square. All four of them marched out, the Rowlands woman leading the way, looking purposeful. She heard something about a nature hike but not one of them looked the part. The Rowlands woman sported some sort of movie star notion of country clothes — a tight fitting gingham dress with a foolish white collar, all starched and stiff, pearl earrings to match. The men had finally given up on suit jackets — Rowlands in shirtsleeves, but still sporting a fancy ivory and brass cane.

Elle watched them from the kitchen window as they meandered past the clearing and down to the trails. A horrid thought crossed her mind and she tried to shut it down. They seemed to be heading in the direction of her last walk with Dog. It was foolish to think they would find the manchineel tree or if they would even know what they were looking at if they did come upon it. Thinking about it threw Elle into a panic, causing her to trail them. She hid behind the tall brush, all the while hoping they didn't turn around to see her behind them. The more she thought about it, the more foolish she felt, so she hoofed it back, thankful that no one turned to see her. Still and all, she was certain they disappeared down the pathway that led to the tree. *Oh, when will they be off with their foolish selves. They have no business in these parts.*

Elle became aware of where they were at all times and it seemed to her they grew more secretive. That evening the lot of them said little to her, went out in the boat, and returned late in the evening, without bothering to let Elle know, so that the dinner set on the counter, covered with linens, uneaten, almost spoiled. And no one even thought to bring anything of use back to her. No chance for ice or fuel unless she begged for it.

Three days they were here now, and there seemed a natural tempo to Elle's day — at daybreak, she went off to her little shack to feed the chicks, stretch Cat, and check on the plants; then back to the lodge to make up breakfast for the Rowlandses' party, and wash up. By far the chore she resented the most was cleaning out their rooms, something usually left to the charwoman at high season. Sometime around noon, she would prepare snacks and drinks, set up the dinner, and wait till they were down for a nap in the afternoon before she'd feed the chicks again and check on the sacks of soil once more to see if any tomato seedlings were up.

That morning she rigged an automatic watering device made from flannel that hung down into buckets. The flannel wicked just enough water to keep the bottom of the sacks damp enough to feed the thirsty seedlings. But she could not enjoy her own cleverness for long because she was certain a new problem would arise from the most unlikely direction.

Was Billy sending them messages, directing their gaze to where he lay hidden? Would the morning tide wash his torso in when they took a stroll on the wharf?

After tending to the small homestead, she moved quickly, casting her eyes downward whenever she looked toward the tangle of trees. Elle wondered if the Rowlands woman knew exactly where the land was that she thought she had purchased or, even if she cared a fig for it. *A real dough-head, that one.* Still and all, she would not take any chances. Best to let well enough alone.

32

Later that afternoon, the yacht took off with the two men on it, going off to see who-knew-what, leaving the women inside the cabin to battle the heat and the insects that were at their worst in September. A large, white heron landed on a tree branch while Elle was out and about feeding the animals and tending to Cat, stretching his back legs and cleaning his eye wound.

The heron made loud trumpeting noises around the drowned tree roots that hid Billy's bloated remains..

Spooked, Elle could not take the chance that Billy's remains would stay put, especially after being in water a good six or seven days. She had not been afforded a moment's peace since the Rowlandses' circus had descended upon her.

Water lapped gently, knocking the small boat against the wharf in an uneasy tock-tock rhythm, as if calling out to her to get the job done. Elle dried her hands on her trousers, made her way to the wharf, and took a long look around. Seeing no one, she lowered herself into the boat and pushed off the pier with an oar.

The heron flapped his wings and went in for a clumsy nosedive somewhere in the mangrove tangle. Lucky that she spotted this while the party was away—not that a single soul amongst them was the slightest bit enchanted with the flora and fauna that abounded.

The light diminished near the copse, and the trees formed a labyrinthine puzzle. Elle looked hard, trying to tell which roots would hold her weight and which would give. New leaves had sprouted over the past few days, obscuring the metal chains that held the traps below.

She tossed the painter around a slender trunk and could have sworn that the small grove had drifted further out, now forming an island as far away as it could get. No way Elle could shimmy across the shore to Billy's remains. The boat bobbed carelessly as she pulled herself up by grasping a thick trunk and gained a footing on the confusion of slime-covered roots. Finally, she spied a thick chain glinting in the water and let out a relieved breath. She pulled the buoyant trap up with such force that the great heron let go a honk, causing her to scream, the echoes ricocheting around her, circling the island.

She composed herself, surprised by her own foolish outburst. When nothing happened, she sat back on the hummock and mentally located the other chains. After all were accounted for, she methodically pulled up the first few, having only the two remaining when the heron returned, likely drawn by the stench of the crabs now out of water. Elle could not remember them ever smelling this bad and they brought visions of the carnage in Islamorada to mind. The boat rocked unsteadily when Elle placed the large traps inside, trying to balance them and leave enough room to fit in the middle. Only one more and then she could be off.

She had a chain in her hands, when, to her horror, she spotted the unmistakable silhouette of Mrs. Rowlands watching her from the bank. Silently, Mrs. Rowlands had moved in as close as the retreating land would allow. But it was close enough for Elle to make out her expression, intense and unafraid.

Elle gasped, eyes wide with fear.

"G'wan, pull it up." Mrs. Rowlands said, her voice calm and triumphant.

Elle could not respond for a moment, terrified at being spotted and fearful of what might be at the bottom of the pot. She cast her eyes inside and the pot was thick with blue crabs, some with amputated limbs. She would have to pour them out to see what was there.

"You caught me." Elle spoke without thinking.

"Caught you? What's in there?" She was looking intently at the crab pot as she spoke.

Panicked, Elle grasped for words. "My secret crabbing place. Come see for yourself." Mrs. Rowlands hesitated then moved in closer across the unstable land. Elle knew that she would soon be up to her knees in water and would start screaming. Elle reached into one of the traps, pulled a crab out, and tossed it at the woman, who let out a shriek that caused much wing flapping. The heron honked, a small flock of ibis flew away, and Charlie began clucking from afar.

"It's not the end of this. I promise you," the woman yelled, but Elle smiled as she caught the note of terror scarcely hidden in her voice. She had put up with just about enough from her. From the pathway, Mrs. Rowlands pointed a finger at her and yelled. "Something wrong with you. I know you're up to something. Plain as the nose on your face."

Elle tossed the crab pot into the boat, upending it and spied what looked like a long bone, stripped completely clean. The woman was gone, back to the lodge, and Elle moved in quickly, bringing up the last trap, emptying it to find that many of the bones were missing. The ones that remained were well gnawed, and she wondered if the smaller bones had been completely devoured by the hungry crabs. Maybe the tiny bones had slipped through the slats of the traps or maybe they were small enough for the crabs to eat, she thought, pushing the grisly image away.

She crammed the small pile of bones into the last of three large traps and paddled back to the pier. Crabs were loose in the boat and she rowed quickly, eyeing the path to the lodge, looking for unwelcome guests. She was encumbered by the large traps teetering unsteadily, threatening to topple overboard. Crabs scuttled over her legs and one made it overboard by climbing onto a loose board and launching itself over the side.

She took the small boat to the front end of the pier and swung the pot with Billy's bones so that it landed in the water at an angle, moving under the pier. Fully dressed, Elle jumped in after it, and she threaded the long rope through a pipe under the pier, tying it at a taut, sharp angle that she imagined wouldn't be seen by a passing boat.

Once she swam to the surface, it dawned on her how little she resembled her former self, how unafraid she now was of the water. *Think. Think,* she commanded herself. *Think or you will get caught.* Elle stood on the wharf, calming herself as she counted steps to the edge. Twenty steps heel-to-toe from the edge of the pier to the rope with bones.

She repeated this twice more so she would remember.

Twenty steps
heel-to-toe
from the edge of the pier
to the rope with bones

Now that the Rowlands woman had spotted her, Elle would have to wait until the lot of them left before she dared hunt for Billy's torso. She was soaking wet, unable to remove her clothes, jittery from the comings and goings of the lodge's visitors. Like a bad penny, the fishing party showed up just when Elle was about to jump back into the boat. She longed to upend the boat and toss the crabs back into the drink, wanting nothing to do with eating them, knowing full-well where they had been and what they were made up of.

But the captain had his scope out and seemed to be peering directly at her. Before they were within easy eyeshot, she heard the fool lot of them whooping it up on deck. They had a large block of ice with them and a couple boxes of supplies. There was not a thing Elle could do about the crabs, now clawing their way up the sides and into water.

The longer the crabs were in open air, the more putrid they smelled, like dirty skivvies and sulfur. Elle watched them move like battling wind-up children's toys and found her mind wondering which had fed on what parts of Billy. She felt lightheaded and dizzy and had to crouch on the wharf, unable to move for fear of vomiting.

The sky was the color of a flock of spoonbills, and as the dazzling white and silver boat lurched steadily toward her, she grabbed hold of her head with both hands to stop her ears from ringing. Finally, she sat cross-legged in a puddle of water, her head between her legs. The change in blood flow stopped her from passing out, just in time to hear the ever-louder drunken ravings of the banker and one of the fishermen.

"Whatcha got there, missy? You look a sight. Will you get a load of all them crabs!" It was the lazy fisherman, the drunkard, speaking. "I knew you would come through for the guests, Elle. I told them you knew what you were about." He looked at the two men and patted the banker on his back. "See, what'd I tell you!" he said, beaming at the man like a fool, one side of his face beet red, probably from laying down for a snooze on deck. "Now you will see for yourself why people come from far and wide just to sample Miz Elle's famous crab chowder."

The younger fisherman sprinted out of the boat, helping Mr. Rowlands up, handing the husband his cane. Then he disappeared and returned with a folding cart. He tried to hand it to Elle, but this time she did nothing to help. "You alright, Miss? You fall in the brine?"

No, no, I am not all right. I cannot look upon those bodies.

"Elle, here. Let me help you."

"Crabs no good. Got to put them back," she said.

Mr. Rowlands looked down at Elle. "Not you, too. You been tippling? You too?"

Elle stared around her at the activity. The younger fisherman was flinging the crabs into the cart. Elle knew she would have to master her feelings, so she did what she knew best to do. She refused to think of it, grabbed what part of her shirt she could get hold of, and wrung out the water, but it had already begun to dry. A body never stays wet here for long. Sun too bright and greedy.

She started to move her limbs and focus on the chore at

hand. Rowlands, too old, and the banker and fisherman, too drunk to be useful. No one stirred to fetch the bags and ice so she moved toward them, her long habit of using hard work to get past unpleasantness coming to the fore. She remembered what her aunt said to her after her mother passed: "It gets better, Elle, but first it gets worse." Her mother's passing had seemed too much to bear at the time, and Elle couldn't see past her grief. Just on the cusp of womanhood, she tried to understand the words her aunt had spoken, but she wouldn't know the true meaning of them until later. Now things have been getting only worse, she thought. Will they ever get better?

It took a few minutes for her wits to catch up with her limbs, so without thinking much about it, she moved onto the large boat to get the second folded trolley. "I'll get the ice and you bring the crabs around to the lodge," she said. "Thanks be for that second cart." The three men laughed nervously, mildly embarrassed at being caught shirking their rightful share of the work and leaving it for a woman to handle.

The one sober fisherman looked annoyed. "Don't know why you took them out of the pots. So much easier to handle in the traps. Now someone's got to make a second trip to bring the traps back of the lodge."

Elle ignored the comment and pushed her cart out of earshot, down the pier to the back of the lodge, beating the men by a good few minutes, looking about her for signs that the storm might not have cleaned up. She hadn't returned to the fish-butchering place since the storm and felt relief that the rain had washed away all traces of the blood-soaked grounds. By the time she loaded a good chip of ice into the zinc box in the kitchen, she heard the sound of traps being stacked by the icehouse.

The land had already begun to form a crust, and Elle knew it would soon be dry and hard as usual. She would have to summon the muster to work in this spot again, to put the memory in her back pocket if she wanted to eat.

She peered around the corner, nodded her thanks, and brought out the large-ring kerosene cooker. Then she ladled water from a bucket into the large pot and lit the fire beneath it. Last place she wanted to be was alone in the fish-butchering place, but there was nowhere else to steam the crabs. If she cooked crab on the stove in the lodge kitchen, the smell would linger for weeks.

Elle dropped the crabs into the pot, sometimes missing it altogether, for she could barely manage to look upon them. No way she could shove them back into the traps. They would not willingly go through the narrow opening, and there were far too many to use up, what with no ice in the icehouse and no telling when more would come.

She boiled them, a half dozen or so at a time, tossed them on the table, then did another batch, and another. They just didn't seem to diminish, there were so many of them. She seemed to have been at it forever, her mind running down crab cake recipes, thinking on how she would need the pliers to pry the legs off and scissors to open them and scrape out the tiny bits of flesh, and how many hours of work were in front of her. Darn that drunken sailor. It used to take her half a day to prepare the sweet meat and then only if she could borrow another pair of hands for the shelling.

In her haste to finish the job, she turned quickly and jerked the cart with live crabs closer to her and it keeled over, spilling a good number of them over the side before she could right it. They made a break for it, taking off in all directions, unnaturally speedy, as if they knew their fate. Elle yelled for help, but no one bothered to answer her cries. A few crabs scurried behind the concrete posts that held the icehouse. Others made it to the bush to lay low and still.

The fishermen had already left for the boat, so when no one came to Elle's aid, she began to see the entire debacle as comical and tossed another batch into the pot, crowding out the others and making the water boil over. She took her large, slotted spoon out near the shed and icehouse and began calling to them. "Here boy, come to mama, you little so and so." She laughed, cackling in a high-pitched voice as she bent to peer under the shack. From behind, she caught the tail end of a whispered conversation and straightened up in time to see the Rowlands woman and her poor, beet-red husband. The whispered word *crazy* hung in the air, till the woman turned tail and headed back for her cabin.

Later that evening, much as she tried not to find too much pleasure in it, Elle couldn't help enjoying the sight of that smug party spoon great slurpfuls of crab chowder into their jaded gullets, all the while smiling their approval. She wiped her eyelids on her good, green-flowered apron and checked her hair—nice and flat on top in a matching green bandanna—and watched Blanche Rowlands, that woman, scarf her soup down like a sailor rescued from starvation and being lost at sea.

Together at last, you 'n Billy, together at last. She almost wanted to hum it as a song. "Got some crab cakes for you tomorrow, if you're not sick to death of crab by then."

"Can't imagine I would ever get sick of these. Just as sweet as they can be and, I must admit, they are right about your talents." The old man had recovered and he made a slight gesture, discretely pointing his spoon toward his bowl, which Elle recognized as a polite way to ask her for a second helping. When she returned with it full, he said, "Have some yourself. My dear mother once told me never to trust a cook who will not sample her own fare."

"Very kind of you, sir, but oh, no, never, until everyone is gone," Elle said, mimicking a small curtsy as she had been taught by the owners. She placed the bowl in front of him. From the corner of her eye, she spied something gray and shiny bobbing in the middle of his bowl. With horror, she realized it was the tip of a finger.

It sat there, Elle staring at it for a second, hardly believing what she was looking at. Mrs. Rowlands's eyes followed hers to the finger and before the old man could find his glasses, Elle whisked the bowl away, heading fast for the kitchen. Mrs. Rowlands moved quickly, her chair screeching on the linoleum, and Elle knew she was hot on her heels. Before Mrs. Rowlands could stop her, Elle snatched the finger from the bowl and swallowed it.

"What the bejesus are you doing?" Mrs. Rowlands yelled.

Elle heard the old man yell something. Ignoring Mrs. Rowlands entirely, she said, in a shrill, high voice, "seasoning, sir, it needs seasoning."

"You ate it!" Mrs. Rowlands yelled.

"What. What are you talking about?"

"It was a finger. You ate part of a finger!" Mrs. Rowlands's voice was shrill.

"You're crazy. You have a wild imagination. I did no such thing."

"Omigod. Is that what you did? Is that what you did to Billy? You put him in the crab traps!"

Elle walked swiftly back into the dining room, but Mr. Rowlands was already up, apologizing to Elle for his wife's outburst.

"I see it all the time," Elle said. "This place not for everyone." She nodded sympathetically at the other couple. "Can drive a body to distraction." She smiled stiffly and they nodded back then stared at their empty bowls, confusion and worry on their faces.

33

Next morning, Elle woke early, went to the ruined chicken coop, found seven eggs, got scraps of spam, and baked a regal breakfast pie for everyone, even opening a precious jar of stewed tomatoes to celebrate their impending departure. They sure could put it away, despite their so-called manners.

Finally, they returned to their cabins, leaving Elle alone in the kitchen. She finished cleaning the last pan and doused the stove, then heard low voices out the open window. The chartered boat was docked at the stone landing by the lodge, waiting, ready to take them far, far away. Elle walked quickly to the small, oddly silent group. Without asking, she reached for the older woman's case and trunk then told the party to wait while she retrieved a large cart. Neither of the two fishermen saw fit to help them with their ungainly parcels and large leather bags. Without embarrassment or explanation, they dropped the luggage on the spot and headed off toward the pier. Elle carefully piled everything onto the cart. Within minutes, she was hot and sticky and although the load was fairly heavy, she enjoyed lugging it to the pier, her spirit lighter by the minute, eager for them to finally be off.

When she arrived, not a single soul offered her so much as a nod of thanks. Elle spied Cat, awakened from a snooze, skulking about in the small rowboat. When the light hit his bad eye, she noted it healing, nicely scabbed over. Elle left the parcels in the cart and moved toward the boat, and was about to call for the men to get a move on and load their things. Mrs. Rowlands trailed behind her, walking awkwardly on her high heels. Old Man Rowlands stopped to lean over the pier. He looked put upon, obviously bothered by the heat. The other couple stopped, and the three of them spoke in low murmurs that Elle did not bother to try to overhear.

She moved away from the threesome, only stopping at the end of the pier. Elle imagined Billy's bones swinging gently in the trap underwater—the last part of his long goodbye—exactly where she was standing. Only good thing was that the Rowlands woman had not bothered her after she snatched the finger from the soup. Husband had nothing to say about it. Probably wise on his part. She heard heels hard on planks and knew the woman was at her.

"So where is he?"

She never gives up, does she? Elle knew exactly whom she was talking about. She felt like she had been waiting for this question all the while they were at the lodge. Still, it was something she knew she would have to juggle.

Mrs. Rowlands spoke again. "I want to know what happened to Billy."

Elle, not expecting her to get to the point so quickly, was surprised at the bluster of the woman. But, for all that, she was nothing but fluff and sham.

"What do you mean?"

"Never made it to the ferry, did he? You saw to that." Her old man was far down the pier, and Mrs. Rowlands gestured at him to stay where he was.

"I know nothing of the sort," Elle answered. Her skiff rocked alongside, hitting the pier regularly. Cat stood alert at the helm, eyeballing the two of them. Elle willed someone to come walking down the pier. Conversation was getting too close for her taste.

Elle spoke again. "I got neither the time nor the inclination to talk to you."

Mrs. Rowlands's usually perfect red lipstick had bled in the heat, and she looked the image of a carnival clown— frilled collar, face plastered with pale, cracking powder. Elle scrutinized her openly.

"Don't know how you manage to get around in those." Elle looked at her open-toed shoes, her sandals she called them. She whistled. "Must take some kind of special training."

Elle knew she was tempting fate but could not resist goading the woman. She wanted nothing more than to knock the smug look off the woman's face. Who is she to come blundering into my life, making trouble?

"I watched you from the ferry," Mrs. Rowlands said in a low voice.

"What ferry?"

"The morning of the storm. When we went out on the last ferryboat. You know what I'm talking about, don't you?" Before Elle could respond, Mrs. Rowlands continued, "By the small island, in the trees. You were there and I saw you. Made a very odd picture—you ducking so no one could call you to the boat and Billy nowhere in sight."

"And what concern of it is yours, what goes on between

a husband and wife?" Elle said.

"Two can play at that game, missy. Wouldn't you like to know what I am up to around here in this ungodly season? What we are up to, I should say."

The ridiculous woman wanted to get a rise out of her and would enjoy nothing more than to lure her into a down and dirty catfight, brawling it out so she could act the wounded grand dame in the end. It was something Elle could not win, and she knew it. They were four, and she one, and it would be like that if she was to get into it. If she could only hang on, they would be off before she knew it.

"I done what I could to keep your gang happy. Can't seem to be doin' much more, what with the lack of ice. Not much entertaining for what you must be accustomed to."

"Don't play coy with me. We've been through all that before, missy. We are certainly not here for the food, if you can call it that."

"I know you was fond of Billy. Wanted to help him out, and the two of us, Billy and me, appreciated it, we did. And I do beg pardon for the simple fare."

The Rowlands woman was getting pinched about the eyes. "Like I said, I didn't come here for the amenities."

No, nothing I can provide, Elle thought. *I know exactly what you came here for, and with the old man in tow, you brazen chippy.*

"Well, what did you come here for?" Elle put on her best country bumpkin look, stared at the woman's unnaturally white face, imagining her own, ruddy and rawboned.

Although she wouldn't answer, Elle could tell she was not all bluff. Had she been at the crabbing place? Could she know more than she was letting on? Could she have found

Billy's torso? No, that woman couldn't keep counsel if she stubbed her painted toe, so she would never have kept it to herself. She didn't have it in her.

Elle looked straight at her but got no response, Mrs. Rowlands's mouth as tight as a miser's purse.

"You sure had it bad for him, I gotta say," Elle said.

"What?"

"You musta liked him an awful lot. Never no tellin' what makes a person goofy."

Mrs. Rowlands let out breath and paused. Finally, she spoke. "A war vet like that, after all he gave. He had no business being that down and out." Elle heard genuine anguish in her voice. But Mrs. Rowlands caught herself and said, "Almost a big brother to me."

Least that dumb Palooka's got someone to mourn for him. Elle's mind skittered from one part of the island to the other. For a passing moment, she almost thought she would have been better off if the fool was alive. *All that hell for nothing.*

"We plan to turn that hovel into proper storage for fishing and other gear for Mr. Rowlands." She was pointing at Elle's house when she spoke. "It has the bones of a decent sized closet once we rid it of the debris accumulated over the years."

"Oh, no. That place is mine."

"We'll see," Mrs. Rowlands said and turned to leave, her high heels hammering the polished planks.

Elle stayed at the far end of the pier and watched her lead the party back to the lodge. She looked at the pompous rooster leading her three little hens back to the lodge. They must be waiting for the ferry; Elle wished it would finally arrive and put an end to this farce.

Alone, she thought back on when she first learned about

how the land on No Name was divvied up. Everything south, except this one small parcel between the pier and the lodge, belonged to No Name Lodge.

North was the wild and unspoiled domain of the hermit. But the hermit was smart enough to keep that bit of land close to the wharf so he could easily get his crops to market without having to beg permission. So he gave her title to it after she gave him the extra money she got for his tomatoes. That was the only time she saw a thin smile cross his miserly features. So long as she helped him store and load his harvest, she was welcome to it. Other than that, he had no use for land that spilled onto the busiest place on the island, the walkway directly off the pier where he would not be able to avoid dealing with people. Visitors to the lodge had to pass through the outskirts of the half-acre property — no way to dodge them — passing by the cistern, which was now Elle's small, unfinished house, barely hidden from view by a grove of palms and pigeon plums. She had earned it fair and square, her one room house that had proved its mettle in the storm, able to withstand heavy rain and wind, being made of steel-reinforced concrete.

But now that was in jeopardy — dragging the hermit into her battles and finding out what her rights were when she thought all had been settled with a nod, a handshake, a paper now torn in half.

Elle stood on the pier, in the sun, unable to move her mind from the field with plants that hadn't come into bearing, tomatoes scarcely up, knowing that what she would get for them was a paltry sum. No, without her job, she would be forced out of No Name and wouldn't stand a chance in Key West. She had no desire to join the legions of shattered souls sleeping in alleys till some sort of pestilence befell her. She had no kin left to turn to, no relatives that she would have to serve. Better to be a slave to strangers than your own kind, she thought, reminded of the way her uncle had treated her when her mother had passed. Truth be told, she knew not a single, friendly soul with means.

As she looked at the mess of trunks laying abandoned on the pier, oppressive thoughts came to her unbidden — the tree, the apples, a way out. She briefly wished she had the moxie to make better use of the fruit of the manchineel. Elle came face-to-face with what remained of her chances and she decided, finally, that she had to leave No Name, for good. There was no use fighting for something she would only lose in the end.

Once the cursed Rowlandses' party left, she would make her way out of this inhospitable place. It was that or what the fates had in store for her, to give in to her own rage and frustration and become another Billy, weighted down with bitterness and dreaming of revenge.

34

On the walk back to the lodge, Elle pondered her fate, unable to come up with a workable plan to survive under the lash of the Rowlands woman. She spent the dwindling money seventeen different ways in her mind, but the once princely sum now looked mean and sparse.

The ferry sounded in the distance. Nothing was dependable any longer; the boats came haphazardly ever since the storm.

The sight of Monty waving at her from the helm cheered her somewhat. He greeted her with warmth, happy to meet an old friend, or maybe just pleased at his routine returning. He was decked out in new white and blues, but for all his polish, he looked thin and bruised behind the eyes. When asked, he said he wasn't sure the ferry would continue to stop at No Name on a regular basis, but Elle didn't want to hear of any more loss.

"Makes no never mind to me anyhow. Less work is all."

"So whaddya think of the Rowlands woman?" she asked him, hoping for a little light-hearted banter. Nothing Monty enjoyed more than sizing up a woman to an appreciative audience.

"Wouldn't get anywhere near a dough head like that. Wouldn't be no fun at all. Reckon she would make you do all the work, if you know what I mean. Dangerous."

"What makes you think that? Seems to me most red-blooded men would like to have a go at her if they could."

Monty shook his head from side to side. "This place must be getting to you. Never did know you to go on like that before. Always saw you as a lady."

"You kidding me? Take a good look, mister." Elle spread out her arms, glared at him.

"Not the clothes what makes the dame, either way. I know what I'm looking at alright."

Elle's arms dropped and she stared at the scrub around her feet. "Don't know if that's exactly true."

"What's that supposed to mean?" Monty inched away from her and Elle understood that he wasn't much for confidences. Must have been a good lot of females try to lean on him in past days. "You ever been married?"

"Nope. Nothing official, but I've had my share of hard knocks, if that's what you mean. Know enough not to get on the wrong side of a woman with a mission."

"You mean me?"

"You? No. I thought we were talking about the Rowlands woman. But that is not my affair. Not the same for you, Elle. I know that, and more than I care to say as well." Monty took Elle's hands in his own. "I'm not going to spoon feed it to you, Elle. Seems you got a hankering to know."

"Tell me," she said.

But Monty wasn't listening. He was on a roll, speaking fast, as if to convince himself that it had to finally be out in the open. "Might be what you need to...go on and finally put Billy's ghost to rest. Billy was not the man you thought him to be. He never..."

Before he got any further, the Rowlandses' party had made their way back to the pier, the men each carrying another trunk. They struggled with the last of their small loads, annoyed at the lack of help.

Monty spoke quickly. "You must have figured out how it is. I don't really gotta tell you about Billy and Blanche, do I?"

This was the first time Monty used Mrs. Rowlands's first name, and it struck Elle as ludicrous and perfectly suited to the woman.

"Blanche," Elle whistled. "Imagine that."

Mr. Rowlands, beet-red and puffed up from the short walk in the scorching sun, addressed Monty. "Sir, would you please alert the Captain that we intend to leave as soon as possible." He looked from Monty to her, removed his straw boater, nodded at Elle to approach as if he were some great potentate instead of the dupe she saw sweating it out on her turf. When she didn't move, he approached her, put a few bills in her hand, then folded her fingers over the money. "We are very grateful for all your hard work and certainly hope you will stay on in some capacity when the establishment changes hands."

Mrs. Rowlands (or Blanche, as Elle now preferred to think of her) cut in. "We'll see, daddy, we'll see. Let's not be too hasty to make promises we can't keep."

"Too true, for a promise made is a debt unpaid, as my good mother always told me."

For the first time, Elle was curious about the couple with the Rowlandses. It seemed to her that they barely spoke, just nodded and smiled whenever either of the

Rowlands moved an inch.

"And when would that be, sir?" Elle dared to ask.

Mr. Rowlands shushed his wife, probably catching wind of her look of outrage that Elle would dare ask for information not voluntarily proffered. "Hush, Blanche. The woman has a right to make preparations." He nodded at the couple. "Well, Henry says we ought to be able to wrap up this deal in a month or so, and he ought to know; he's my banker." With that he laughed, as if it was some grand joke, and a good time would be had by all.

Mrs. Rowlands's silly-looking white straw hat seemed strangely askew, perched on her head at a severe diagonal, making Elle want to ram her head through it and turn it into a collar. No doubt it was someone's fool notion of fashion. A runaway hat ribbon, long enough to wrap around her throat a couple of times, good and tight, snaked in the breeze. Elle watched the ribbon with a sinister expression.

"What in heaven's name are you staring at?" Blanche turned from glaring at Elle to softly smiling at her husband, one hand on her hat, her face a strumpet's come-on. "Go ahead, dear, ask her. I mean, remind her of what we have decided, about the deed.'

Old man Rowlands cleared his throat and began. "My wife had opportunity to purchase a small parcel of land, in fact, the land that we are now standing upon—a third of an acre—that we will need to make a road leading straight to this pier. She says you want to hang on to it for some reason."

"Land's mine. And it's a half acre, not a third."

The woman reached into her purse and pulled out a small, folded paper. "Here's what's left of the deed. I believe you have the other half."

Elle wanted to snatch it out of her hand and shred it to pieces. The old habit of confronting situations that she had little chance of winning came back to her. In the early days, when Billy first started hitting her, she would stand, unmoved, surly and defiant, and keep coming up for air like a weighted clown at a carnival. She never had enough sense to know when she was bested.

"Not your land. It's mine. Got it from the hermit."

"Hermit owned this land?"

"That's right, the hermit still owns more'n half of No Name Key. Gimme that paper. Let's have a look at it." Elle reached out to snatch the paper, a phony smile on her face, but Blanche turned and slowly folded the paper and placed it back in her purse.

Surely they knew there was no reasoning with the hermit. He would rather perish than give up any of his property and had a terror of people encroaching on his private space. Wasn't even keen on animals, from what she'd been told. Only living thing he had any use for was the land. He denied love to whatever walked and talked and grunted and wheezed, but he poured it into his plants, doing things so wondrous that even first rate Florida growers came courting to learn his secrets. Legend had it that he had kept the great grower, Krome himself, outside his shack, making him cool his heels and return twice before he would see him.

"Why would he give you land?"

"Maybe he finds me more useful than most." *Fools can't imagine beyond their own nose.* Elle stared at this woman, no longer amazed at how brazen she was, leaning on the man she had cuckolded not a week before, having the cheek to challenge her right to a shack she herself had no earthly use for. "Maybe some of us have to earn our keep fair and square." Elle aimed her words at Blanche.

"She can't talk to me that way. I won't let her." Blanche moved forward and slapped Elle hard in the face. And Elle's long years of holding her own counsel, coming and going at the whim of others, struggling for a small corner of a barren land, threatened to burst her chest. She vowed that this woman would not win. It was she or the woman, but she would no longer go down easy. Her hands, now arranged into two perfect semi-circles that could form a noose around Blanche's throat, returned, with great effort, to her sides.

The men said nothing, having no understanding of what they viewed as the incomprehensible laws of womankind.

Finally, Monty stepped in and began to make excuses for Elle, speaking fast. "She just lost her husband and now you threaten her job. I've known Elle many years now, and, with all due respect, sir, you would regret losing her. Her key lime pie and crab chowder is famous all through the Keys."

Blanche, her head at an unnatural angle, her hat barring in the way, moved toward her husband and soon had him ensnared in a clinch.

Old man Rowlands extricated himself from her grasp, cleared his throat, and knocked his cane on the ground twice. He spoke in an oddly formal tone, "Madam? Miss Elle, I am giving you fair warning that we are in negotiations to buy this place and you need to seek another situation. We will be bringing our own cook from Philadelphia when we return. There is simply not enough live-in work for two."

"What about a helper, a second cook?" It was Monty. Elle was too flabbergasted to interrupt him.

Blanche answered him. "Well, if the second cook comes

with a general handyman, maybe." She turned to address her husband. "Elle's husband, name of Billy Woodman, was so useful when we were last here. Remember, daddy? Mr. Woodman is a veteran of the Great War and you know how I feel about that." She turned to address Elle. "If he is agreeable, then we can hire you both—he as a driver-handyman, and you as a second cook and all-around helper." She looked back to her husband. "Don't you think?"

Before he could answer, Elle spoke. "This land is mine and I'm telling you it for the last time. Seems like no one wants to hear the truth of what I have to say."

"I'll show her the deed with Billy's...Mr. Woodman's...signature. Now that I have witnesses."

Everyone leaned in as Blanche snapped open her small, hard purse. Her red nails glittered in the sun like diamond-shot blood as she held the parchment for Monty to read.

His mouth hardened into a horizontal line and he shook his head, sadly. "Looks like Billy's signature alright. I know it from the ferry rides. Sorry, Elle."

"I told you. We bought it fair and square."

Mr. Rowlands patted his wife's arm and nodded. "Yes, yes. Of course you did, dear."

"This property is mine. He had nothing to do with it. I bought it with my own money. He didn't spend a nickel on it," Elle countered, fear and anger swelling in her heart.

"Don't matter. It's communal property. Either one of you have the right to do with it as you like."

Elle looked up at a couple of turkey buzzards circling above her. You don't have ahold of it yet, she thought, lips pressed together like a rat trap.

I still have a month to straighten it out with the hermit, Elle thought, although being in the right meant nothing in the Rowlandses' world.

Finally, and mercifully, Monty and the boys sounded the horn and the Rowlands couple and their party took off, ribbons trailing, brass glinting off their trunks, and the old man's ivory walking stick put away in favor of a high-polished redwood deal that seemed more of a bother than an aid on this terrain.

Good luck getting any say-so here, buddy-boy, Elle thought. He tightened his hold on Blanche's arm, which seemed to Elle to be gaining in girth the more the man dwindled. Wouldn't take much sun to shrink him a size or two and little again to dry him up entirely.

In fact, as Elle walked away, she stole one last look at them, Mrs. Rowlands hulked over the old man, pushing him down with plenty of backbone behind the gentle press of her hands, like a carny clown cranking an overdressed monkey.

35

Over the next few days, Elle made a mental note of everything she needed do to regain claim to the property. First order of business was to ask the hermit and the pastor if she could do anything about Billy's signature. But she knew in her heart that the pastor would be on the side of the Rowlandses and that the hermit would want nothing to do with the dealings of man.

Terror at diving for Billy's torso paralyzed her. As days flew by, Elle avoided the pier, always thinking of what lay dangling in the water below. First, she would lose the house and the small purchase she had on No Name. Then she would be tried as a murderess in Key West—and for killing a war vet, at that.

Her mind sashayed out to the crab traps and beyond, past the place where the groves had been, into the wood where the hermit lived. Elle had never actually been there. She heard gunshots ring out from time to time when she was out running with Dog and imagined him going after some critter or maybe killing something to eat. But when she actually thought about it, she couldn't come up with anything that he would have to shoot. Oh well, maybe it was gun practice.

The few times the hermit met her, he seemed to take pains to gentle his face. But it was always his call to meet her; she never sought him out. Maybe that was why they got along. Elle knew he had some sort of arrangement with school kids in Big Pine. They would come down, pick the key lime trees clean, and get the fruit shipped out. You could tell who those kids were by their scratched up arms and hands, even with long sleeves. Key limes are half the size and twice the bother of any other limes—trees with the nastiest spikes hide the juiciest fruit—so small it takes great numbers of them to make any real profit. And until key lime pie came into style, no one knew what to make of the harvest.

Cat pawed at her, making her aware that she was frowning while she mentally drew an invisible pathway to the hermit's house, to where everyone said it was. But she knew not one single soul who had been inside.

Elle moved behind the row of palms and a giant boulder that formed a curtain between the cistern and the pier, and stared into nothing. Cat came to lie in her lap. Charlie and the hens clucked at her, and when she finally paid attention, she saw that one of the baby chicks had died, the water she left for them dank and soiled from its carcass.

Elle removed the dead chick, changed the water, and fed every one, her limbs heavy and pinging all at the same time. The black and white speckled hen fled from her chicks and jumped manically at the wall, as if she was angry and frustrated that one of her babies was dead. Elle gently lifted her back into the corral and the five remaining baby chicks ran under her wings and legs for comfort. Finally, she settled down, clucking softly. Charlie let out a howl then began scratching at the ground as if performing a ritual.

When dusk fell, a large bird swooped down and grabbed another baby chick that had wandered away from the flock. Their grim entangled silhouette rose to circle the treetops frantically, the hawk in search of a place to shred and devour its prey.

That night, uninvited thoughts crammed her brain and she felt like a wraith lifted into the air, tightly held by something bigger and surer than she was. Bright traces and pings of color darted around the insides of her eyelids. Something warm weighted her chest, but it was only Cat, in his favorite place, lying across her chest and throat.

Elle lay in a half-sleep trance, unable to form a thought or plan. She finally threw Cat off her sweat-soaked body and walked through the doorway, dreading the day to come. She thought of what No Name Key looked like from high above, again trying to form a picture of exactly who owned what and where it was. Cat watched her from his perch on a piece of limestone as she picked up a small branch and began drawing in the dirt.

The stick in her hand moved like a divining rod, forming a map on its own, the trail leading to where the hermit lived. When he spoke to her, rather, the few times he did, he sounded like he knew about a lot of things, although his foreign accent made it hard to tell if he was considered a well-schooled man back in his own country. Not once did he look her in the eyes when he spoke, so she followed his lead and cast her gaze to the ground, occasionally sneaking peeks at him when she could. His shoes were heavy, dark leather, with perfectly molded steel toes, like something worn by a character in the funny pages. Whenever she saw him, he was wearing the same pair of heavy overalls and long-sleeved shirt, no matter how hot and sticky it was.

She dug the stick into the loam, gouging out pathways and openings, making wavy lines for water, drawing a childish lodge, finally placing an X where the manchineel tree grew. Then she filled in the groves, the pier, the pastor's house and the store, and some of the homes she knew about.

When she finished, she was surprised at what was left. It seemed the hermit owned more than she supposed. The lodge sat on property bordered by her half-acre spread. Did he really own the land? Elle feared that it might not be his to sell. And she had yet to prove he had actually given it to her. Did he want to keep it as insurance so he could get to the pier from all directions?

He was certainly smart enough to fool everyone. Either way, it was time to find out what she did and did not have and make her plans accordingly. The more she thought on it, the less likely it seemed that Billy had ever met him. What a fool she had been to take him at his word.

Damn the scorpions, I'm goin' for the jar. It seemed to Elle that a castoff jar—an empty jar pilfered from rightful owners who had no more use for the thing—always held her greatest secrets.

Cat sensed that something was up and yowled as Elle moved, springing to the safety of the slab. Elle moved to the corner of her crude little home, counted nine steps, and toed around the spot till she felt some give in the soil. After poking at loose rocks and teasing them out, she pried the jar from its lair and took it inside her house. She had wrapped the cash in the deed, and now she took out the bundle, being careful not to crush the paper.

Although it was daytime, the place was dark and airless

beneath the palm fronds. In a shaft of light, Elle made out
the words "Land Deed" and a number stamped on the far
right side. She was missing the second half but, even to her
eyes, it looked crude and appeared to lack signatures. It
seemed to Elle that these things were usually awash in fancy
letters and plenty of signatures, but this had only one name
on it—the many-syllabled Russian name—and a few words,
in Russian she supposed, signed with obvious formality.
Still and all, it appeared sparser than she remembered. If this
was a sham piece of paper, this deed was Billy's own death
warrant, fool that he was. *Or maybe it will be both of ours.
Guess neither of us figured on that.*

The small space felt more like a tomb than a home and
brought Elle no closer to gaining answers. She stuffed
everything back into the jar, reburied the lot of it, and
walked quickly away, past the thinned sentry of trees that
hid her place from view, and onto the wharf. When she
reached the end of the pier, she imagined Billy's last remains
slung underneath the wood she stood upon and stomped
down hard as if to force his secrets through the wharf. But
he was nothing but bones, slung out of sight, rattling under
the pier.

Her thoughts returned to the hermit and the gift she had
prepared for him in exchange for a way to stay on this small
island. The pile of clamshells and seaweed, cleaned and
fermented proper and cured in the sun, would be garden-
gold to him. He would surely know their worth. She'd made
good use of the sacks of vegetables, half-rotten with no ice to
stave off their demise. Elle had turned the steamy mess
twice a day to coax a perfect stew to feed the hungry soil. In
seasons past, guests complained about the smell, so Elle had
moved the pile near her small place. It didn't bother her at

all but rather foretold a bountiful earth and all things good and rich and ripe.

Now, certain it was ready, she got to work and piled her cart high with vegetables mushy and teeming from heat. She then topped the offensive pile with the sacks that held three-dozen hearty tomato seedlings — her offering to the hermit to soften him up before asking for information about her property.

Elle had gotten ahold of a book in the lodge study that told how No Name formed, and she imagined the tiny bodies of bleached sea creatures that once scuttled across the ocean floor, piled one atop another, their weight finally causing them to peek above the waves. Soon birds would stop to rest and drop seeds, until finally a tree formed, followed by others that decomposed to make soil. The land took shape by chance, moaning and groaning on the backs of small skeletons, millions of tiny bones layered over the ages, the tides pushing it back, pressure clumping it together.

Elle picked up a perfect shell, placing it carefully into a sack with others. She planned to use them to decorate her house once it was completed. Finally, she could dither no longer and looked into the emptiness over the pier. She was completely alone and could loiter no more.

Cat trailed discretely behind her on her way to the hermit's place, though she did what she could to discourage him.

Elle rehearsed the conversation she wanted with the hermit. She would be casual about bringing up the property. She cleared her throat, flattened her hair, and practiced. "Sir," she said out loud. "Do you recall your promise to me about the land and the cistern? Well, I'm living there now but need something to prove it belongs to me." *Stupid, sounds just plain stupid.*

Best be straightforward—he had no talent for small talk, nor talk of any kind, really.

She knew that would mean walking a couple of miles either way, twice a day, to water the tender seedlings in their early stages. If she hoped to find the man's congenial side, she would have to make the trek.

Elle pushed the cart onto the uneven road, and Cat followed, excited at the noise and activity, hiding in brush and then pouncing out at odd angles, almost making her tip the load over once or twice. She stopped to rest. The land looked skimpy, like she was walking atop the balding head of a giant, and she worried for the lime trees and sapodilla groves and tomato beds. She was getting closer to the grove, outlined by the tall trees planted on the perimeter to block out curious eyes and shade the vegetables. It was hard to make out because the storm had shaved the treetops. Headless tree trunks that looked like amputee victims gathering in a loose and wide semi-circle told her it was the right place. Tiring of the game, Cat hopped in the cart and burrowed into a dry part, away from the muck, and went to sleep.

Once through the clearing, Elle could barely tell it was the same place she had tended only a couple of weeks before. Not a single plant had survived and it was impossible to tell if juice still flowed through the slender trunks of whatever key lime trees remained upright.

Elle moved through the large open space, shaken by the unpredictability of nature. How would the hermit survive? But then she remembered that he had been here for decades and saw more than one storm in his time.

She worked throughout the day, loosening up the silt

with a pickaxe, then raking it smooth, laying down the compost. By sundown, there was still no sign of the hermit.

Proud of her work, she would go to him the next day if she managed to finish the planting. She left the tomato plants inside a covered box, under a tree, letting them acclimate to their new home. Tomorrow she would bring another load, water the lot, then go fetch him and say how obliged she felt.

Cat yelled at her to feed him, so she wheeled him home, the cart as light as her spirit when she imagined how pleased the hermit would be at all her hard work. She was bone tired, but her labor couldn't be denied.

Elle dreamt of rose-hued tomatoes and sturdy key lime trees, fragrant with blossoms, growing quicker than she remembered, as if scrambling to reproduce before another storm did them in, they and their progeny. Nectar carried on the wind gave her visions of a large, working orchard, but even in the dreams, she refused to cast her eyes down upon the stingy soil.

Next morning Elle could hardly wait to get moving. After breakfasting on bread and eggs, she made her way back to the field and finally planted the tomato seedlings, stabilizing the tiny plants with mounded earth around them, eggshells scattered on the surface, and a stick with a frond that served as a sun umbrella. She felt edgy, as if being watched, and remembered times past when he had come up behind her so silently even Dog was caught unawares.

After another day with the hermit nowhere in sight, Elle went to where she thought he lived and spotted a large trailer on cement blocks, partly hidden behind browning foliage. It had to be the place. A staircase made of stacked cement blocks teetered up to the front door. Elle knocked, first lightly, then with greater force. She stood still, waiting for activity. She could have sworn he was inside, so she knocked again. Although she felt a vibration, he would not answer the door. She had an envelope with a note inside, asking him to go to the field and see what she had done. Elle imagined him inside, watching her, but refusing to come out. *Just as well*, she thought. *Let him see in his own way, with no one around to interfere.* His florid signature told her that he was probably able to read and write, but she couldn't be sure. Sorely tempted to look inside a window, she resisted, not wanting to ruin her chances.

36

After three days of toil, Elle was eager for news and sore from rough work. She again looked for signs of activity from the hermit. One last try to reach him, and if it failed, she would have to find out where deeds are registered. She remembered signing the paper and giving it back to him. He returned it to her a month or so later. That was all there was to the whole business. All he had required of her was to sign something and that was good enough for Elle. She never brought it up again, just stored the deed where she thought it was safe.

Elle was leery of pressing too hard for details, fearful of the new lodge owners and other things that she could not yet name. Superstitious, Elle did not want to hex her chances, and old habits of avoiding confrontation and conflict might yet be her undoing. That was the whole of her story: wanting to be rid of Billy, but hoping he would leave of his own accord to find the greener pastures he always held over her head. Elle had never been good at taking matters into her own hands, else she wouldn't have married Billy in the first place.

She dug into the stash once again, grabbing ahold of the pickle jar and fingering the ripped land deed. She would get answers today, not leave his doorway until she spoke to him directly. Elle rolled the paper carefully then folded it in half to fit into her neck pouch. A damp, hot wind blew against her body and she pushed away the tiredness, feeling every bit the beggar at the banquet. She would build the house for herself and she would live in it, and the hermit would help her. Doubtless he would hate the Rowlandses and their plans as much as she did.

In the trudge to the hermit's trailer, Elle prepared her speech, forcing her spirits to climb by imagining herself installed in the small house with a proper roof and window to let in the sun. She would still work at the lodge for a spell, directing other cooks, keeping carferee guests sated and entertained, all coming and going without leaving a trace beyond dirty sheets and dishes. Even the owners would be absent for the most part, leaving her time to build up the fruit grove and the tomatoes and, maybe in the fullness of time, she would have stakes in a couple of boats, if she played her hand carefully.

By the time she arrived at the hermit's, she had convinced herself that even if she didn't actually own the small piece of land, he would grant her another, seeing as how unfairly she had been treated and how useful she was to him. She could even move the house if needs be. Cat traveled with her, running on ahead and hiding in trees to spook her. His one, closed eye seemed to constantly wink at her, the two of them in on some sort of joke. *He sure looks the renegade, suited to this place perfectly.*

But when they got close to the area where the hermit's trailer stood hidden, Cat stopped dead on the perimeter of the clearing. He seemed glued behind a bush, spooked and worried, like a single orange feline amongst a crowd of black cats on All Hallows Eve. Elle looked around but saw nothing. Cats are finicky critters, always imagining things, not like a dog that knows for certain when something is afoot. Elle threw a rock down the pathway to distract Cat, but nothing doing. It stayed still, did not move a whisker. So Elle carried on, more annoyed than amused.

Again, she knocked on the door and again, she received no answer. This time she tried to open the door and the latch almost burned her hand, although it was in shadow and should have been cool to the touch. From the corner of her vision, she saw Cat take off into the woods. Certain someone was inside, she pounded on the door and waited, but no one came. She yelled, "Please, sir, I need to talk to you or I would never bother you. It's important and won't take a minute."

Something suddenly came to a stop inside. When she saw the window, she got angry. She had done all that work for him, and dammit, he would hear her out. She leaned sideways as far as she could manage, trying to peer into the window, but it was just out of reach, the angle too sharp to get a bead on the room inside.

Frustrated, she hopped down from the landing and almost left, but then her anger took over. "It's not fair," she yelled into the closed window.

All the underhanded dirty dealings rushed to her in a wave. The Rowlandses would be back before she knew it, the law on their side, money bulldozing her homestead, and she would be off again, in her dirty pants, her body aged a decade from the last couple of year's strife, while the bastards got rich on the next woman's toil.

Elle spied a couple of large, hollow, cement blocks and stacked them against the side of the trailer under the window. Finally, she scrambled up on tiptoes and peered inside. She nearly fell off the thing because he was there, waiting for her, his face staring out, dead-on into hers. He rapped his knuckles on the window and she jumped off the cement block, as if he had slapped her.

He threw the door open and started to rant. "Get out...G'wan! Off with you. Off my property. Now! I'll tell you when I want you back." He stood there, flapping one arm awkwardly while leaning heavily on his cane with the other. His face was as red as the tomatoes she hoped to harvest.

"Didn't mean to interfere. Just want some answers, pure and simple." Elle was surprised at how hurt she felt. She liked the old man, thought of them as kindred spirits of a sort. He had shown her a kindness, appreciated her talents for making things grow. "After what I did for you. Have you seen your fields? All the work I did?"

"I know what you did." He stared at her with eyes the color of sea glass; so pale he might be a blind man. He shook a crooked forefinger slowly at her, his eyes burning white light into her. "I know," he repeated. He pointed at her with his thick, yellow nail, and Elle felt power spin her around. She felt a sharp stab in the small of her back, like an invisible prod, shoving her off the property. When she turned, he drew an 'X' in the sky above her head. It lingered in the air before tumbling down at her feet.

Broken in front of her, on the ground, was an image of Billy, laid to waste, severed on the sawhorse behind the lodge, his head in a basin, eyes looking out toward the hermit's land. The old man knew; he had seen something.

She felt a warm ball, like a festering abscess, form at the bottom of her stomach.

Of course. The hermit would never leave the island. He'd rather perish in a hurricane than be stuck in a crowd with his fellow man. *Could he have been watching from the banks when I sank Billy?*

Elle's mind raced through all the time after the hurricane when they were two of the few survivors left on No Name. Oh yes, he would have had plenty of time to observe her, catch her in the act. Watching her, silent as a cat.

Would he tell? And then a horrible thought dawned on her. Did he find the torso? And if he did, where is it now?

She thought of the gunshots she occasionally heard coming from his side of the island and rumors that he killed someone who once worked for him. She grabbed for the story in her mind. "Wait. Wait. Be fair. All of us have done things we regret."

She felt a gigantic ball of air hit her in the center of her stomach and force her from his property, pushing her faster and faster, making her run through the clearing and onto the pathway, something nipping at her heels all the way, until she made it, breathless, to the lodge. Ribs bruised, injured leg pounding, she sat on the steps with her hands held fast to the sides of her head to stop the blood from rushing. Her brain swelled, her skull feeling as if it couldn't contain it, as if it would explode through her ears, eyes, her mouth, until finally, she began to choke and then cry.

The image of Billy's bones under the pier flashed in front of her eyes. Curse those bones! And she had to rid herself of them now, and then finally be off from this place with her small sum of money. She would find work somewhere else. This place—always giving her some glimpse of paradise—making her work her fingers to the bone, then snatching the promise away just before it came into view.

That was it—she would take the last trap out of the water and dump the cursed bones overboard in deep water near where the army was busy discovering the remains of other victims of the storm. Then she would be rid of this place.

Once the idea took hold, Elle felt certain that it was the right thing to do. Anywhere would be better than this grim island now closing in on her. She would spend one last night setting the place right, getting a note to the owners, thanking them, and doing everything she could to leave in a proper manner. She'd tell them where she was going but then head out in the opposite direction. Maybe she should say that the old hermit gave her the heebie-jeebies, and that would be no lie, no sir.

Cat walked out of the brush, strangely peaceful now, and that gave her the smallest hope, somehow, as animals have a way of doing.

T he sun was high, the water sparkled like a spilled
jeweler's cache, and although the thought sickened her,
Elle resolved to finish the job of pulling those sorry,
tortured bones out of the last trap dancing demented under
the pier. She touched the knot in her middle that now
spewed acid into her gut.

Walking to the pier, as if walking to the gallows, Elle
noted the emptiness of the horizon as she moved to the edge
and counted slats of wood until she reached twenty-five. She
kneeled on the pier, feeling over the side for the telltale rope
she left as a marker.

She tugged at the rope, now sturdy as a steel girder, and
the loathsome thing would not budge. After tugging hard
and long, her palms almost rubbed raw, it finally began to
give way. She stopped a minute to catch her breath, put her
gloves on, and pulled even harder. *Will I spend my entire
earthly existence tugging at ghoulish ropes, bringing in pieces of
the same dead man, over, and over, again? Maybe I should leave
him here*, she thought for a minute, but knew she could not
risk it so long as she was unsure if the hermit actually had

the torso. *Would anyone believe that old crank? And what if he doesn't have the torso?* But she must not take the chance. Not now, not after doing every other little thing.

The trap lifted, became buoyant, then heavier as she forced it, using the large iron eyelet as a pulley and feeling the rough rope through rawhide gloves. Finally, Elle sat, wedging her feet on iron fittings, tears streaming, cursing at the hard luck she had to forever endure, barely recognizing herself. "This place will not defeat me," she said out loud. "Come. Here. Now." After she spoke, the thing popped out of the water, and she eased the tension, as if reeling in a powerful fish, giving and taking, afraid she would break the rope. It came at her, bobbing playfully before sinking again, as if it were little more than a child's lost waterwings, as if it didn't have the whole of her universe rattling around inside, playing checkers with her destiny.

Get on over here, goddammit! And it dipped and careened a delicate do-si-do. She took a good swipe, finally snapping it up with both hands, and pulled it out of the drink. Elle let out a great roar of victory, startling Cat into a yowl of consternation. "Be off with you," she said as she grabbed the trap and popped it onto the wharf.

Finally, she stood over it and opened it up to peer inside. She made out a thick knot of crabs packed tight, probably gnawing on the bones or each other. But no matter how much they tried, even the meanest, bloodthirsty amongst them couldn't completely lay waste to a human bone. She couldn't muster the heart to dump the mess out to see what was left of Billy. It would be the more prudent course to toss the load overboard once out of this unholy place.

She hopped in the boat and pushed off. Cat jumped in

after her. "No," she yelled at him, "you can't come with me," and in her anger she tossed him out the side of the boat. He began to swim wildly, clawing at the water, but his back legs didn't work properly. No matter how frantically he paddled, he could not stay afloat. He sputtered and then went under, his head emerging for a second, then back down, gone. Elle panicked and dove in after him, grabbed his skinny body, and plunked it in the boat. When she climbed in after him, she noticed he lay completely still. She pressed on his chest and finally grabbed his head, put her fingers over his nose, covered his mouth with hers, and breathed air into his tiny lungs a few times till he finally upchucked a load of water on her lap and stood on all fours to shake himself. Elle placed him back on her lap and began to paddle out, filled with gratitude that her small companion was okay. He snuggled in, and she was happy to let him stay so she could watch over him, ashamed of what she was becoming. She patted him a few times, a tear in her eyes, cooing at him while she stroked his ears. "I'm so sorry, so sorry." Her words trailed in the air and Cat settled in close until she picked him up and placed him on a soft towel. Elle was glad to see No Name Key recede into the distance, to hear Cat making his usual noise, growling and purring at the same time.

Elle wouldn't be out of sight of land for a bit, but she was just plain grateful to be away from that place of pain which she had once loved so much. Cat soon woke up and moved farther away from her, proud and cantankerous as ever, though he had no right to be, looking out to sea, his crusted-over eye giving him the appearance of a scrawny four-legged castaway.

Elle began to relax into the ride, engine running low,

with the peace that comes from making a decision. She charted a course in her mind, spending the money by tabulating the price of a fare to the Carolinas, where she thought she would have the best chance of work and make the most use of the small sum she had left. What had been a small fortune a short time before now seemed a picayune sum, what with fares, room and board, and all that. And how she would hate to leave Cat behind. Maybe Mrs. Dean knew of someone who wanted an excellent mouser, though there were not many rodents smaller than a cat on the island. As Elle lost herself in visions of what could be, she and Cat moved silently up the waterway, closing in on the lonely spot where she would dump the ragged bones of Billy Woodman. She hesitated, unable to muster up the courage to look upon him one last time, dreading the grisly chore as much as the fear of getting caught.

Elle's mind flitted from one vision to the next, past and future merging with present. Even if the hermit tried to tell on her, Elle convinced herself that he would not be believed, and she began to gain strength. Soon no one would be able to touch her. Oh sure, there was an outside chance of being found out, of someone believing the hermit but, by then she would be long gone. They might even think he had done it if it came to that. Elle was so lost in her reverie that she forgot how narrow the channel was.

Maybe after she finished this she would return to Grassy Key and see if Q had any more sticks. She deserved some comfort. Then she remembered that the Rowlandses appeared outside the door right after she spread the smoke. Oh well, at least the sticks are a goodly tonic for the nerves.

Once around the slender bend, nearing Vaca Key, Elle made out voices in the distance and veered as far away as she could muster in the tight passageway. She smiled and raised her hand in friendly greeting but her smile turned into a gasp when she heard that voice, the unmistakable whinny of that impossible woman. Blanche Rowlands was here, at Vaca Key. Elle recognized the fancy fishing boat she often hired, now tethered to the wharf.

Elle gunned the engine with so much force that it sputtered and died. She tried to row out but knew they had spotted her. Intuitively, she moved to hide the trap. *What the dilly-o is she doing here? Have I conjured her up for the thinking? Of all the darn bad luck.*

"Well, well, well." Blanche Rowlands stood, fists on hips, the channel too narrow to avoid seeing and hearing her. "Look what the cat dragged in," she pointed to Cat, then raised her finger and aimed it at Elle's face. "What ya got there, Elle?" She mimicked Elle's voice when she spoke.

Elle watched in horror as Mrs. Rowlands's sharp features lit with pleasure. Elle grabbed so tight onto the crab pot that her knuckles turned white.

"What are you up to now?" Her eyes narrowed as she looked down on Elle, whose hands would not follow the simplest command to loosen their grip. "I always knew you were up to something. I asked you a question, missy. What are you hanging on so tightly for? What are you hiding?"

Elle finally let go of the trap at the worst possible moment, just when Mrs. Rowlands glared at it most intently.

"Well, well, well, if it isn't another crab trap. Give me that!" Mrs. Rowlands said.

"You have no right. Get out of my way."

"I know you did him in. I saw you grab the finger from the soup. I saw it and I know what I saw. You give that here or I'll call the Coast Guard."

Elle looked around quickly but no one was there. Elle heard rumors that the Coast Guard set up a temporary outpost on Vaca Key to help with bodies and other floating debris, remnants of the storm's destruction. But the wharf looked deserted. Maybe luck was on Elle's side and no one was there

Mrs. Rowlands began to scream in shrill yelps. "Help! Murderer! Help!"

Elle wanted to sprint out of the boat, grab her by the throat, shut her up and toss her into the drink, but she didn't dare take the chance. Maybe someone would hear them. Someone had to be around. Mrs. Rowlands was incapable of fending for herself. Someone had to handle the dirty work. But where were they? Elle knew from the incident in the mangrove that the woman couldn't swim. Maybe she could hit her head on the wharf and Elle would be found trying to save her. She had to risk it.

Elle moved the skiff alongside the wharf and bolted out, not taking the time to tie it up. Instead of shutting up, Blanche ran down the quay, screaming and wheezing, partly hopping from a broken heel. A squat young man from the Coast Guard appeared on the wharf and Elle turned back, and tried to sprint back into the boat but it had moved a few feet from the dock. *What a fool I am! Why didn't I paddle by and ignore her?*

The man wrestled her to the ground before she could dive after the boat. Mrs. Rowlands was jumping up and down, yelling at the top of her shrill breath, "Murderer! Murderer!" He twisted Elle's wrists behind her and sat on her back, grinding her face into the wooden deck boards. Mrs. Rowlands continued to hop around them, yelling "Murderer! Murderer!" until he finally had to say it.

"Shut up, lady."

Mrs. Rowlands advanced and put her foot less than an inch from Elle's face. "I am making a citizen's arrest. I demand you arrest this woman for murder."

"You sure, ma'am? Murder?"

"That's right, young man. Murder! Check what she has in those traps. I bet she has something in the trap." She moved her foot and Elle felt her hot stare. "Be ready to find another finger, or something worse."

"Ma'am?" he said to Elle, his tone urgent and demanding.

"Sir?" she responded.

"I'm going to let you up if you promise not to run. If I have to catch you again, I'll charge you with fleeing, and I'll be forced to keep you tied up all the way to Key West."

"Key West?"

Key West supplied the only police station within fifty miles. The storm had blown all the others away.

Mrs. Rowlands paced around them and Elle sat up. It was all she could manage not to grab her by the ankles and toss her into the drink. The man kept an eye on the two of them as he pulled in Elle's skiff.

"Don't worry," Elle said. "I'm done. I ain't going nowhere." She sat cross-legged, her chin resting on a bent knee.

It took only a few minutes to tie up the skiff and load the trap and Elle into his more powerful boat.

"What about Cat?" Elle asked.

The man shook his head grimly and Elle began to cry again. Cat was already inside his boat, circling the driver's seat.

"Alright, alright. I guess it can come. No real harm

there."

Elle could tell he liked cats though he tried not to show it. He moved Cat from his seat, handling him gently. Elle was surprised that Cat allowed the man to touch him at all. Out of the corner of her eye, Elle caught him scratching Cat under his chin. Mrs. Rowlands let out a little snort of disgust.

"What's this all about, exactly, ma'am?" he asked Mrs. Rowlands directly.

Elle understood that this man, whoever he was, had no patience for Mrs. Rowlands, although he was obliged to do her bidding.

"Are you questioning my right to make a citizen's arrest?"

"Didn't say that, missus. Just don't want to make a long trip for nothing."

The man looked at Elle, as if for a clue, but she hung her head. He would know soon enough. Why was it that now she gets to meet so many good and decent men? Men who would help her, and more, given half a chance. *Why, oh why was it my fate to have met that devil, Billy Woodman, first?*

Elle began to cry. The one thing she vowed never to do, the thing she hated more than anything. It wasn't the beatings Billy gave that ever did it to her in the end; it was the small, unexpected kindnesses she couldn't take.

"Oh, stop it, you stupid wretch. You killed him and you're going to pay."

"And you lay with my husband, you slut."

"Don't listen to her, she's crazy." Mrs. Rowlands's frantic expression gave Elle a thrill of power. Elle didn't care any longer; she had had enough. She rose and grabbed for the crab traps. *Here he is you dumb slattern; here is your sheik.*

The man stood, silent, while she crouched over the trap, awkwardly flipping it over onto the freshly painted wharf that gleamed in the sun. The man stared intently, and Elle looked over the horizon, waiting for the gasps and shrieks.

Crabs, about two dozen of them, scrambled out then sat stunned on the center of the dock. Elle banged on the trap, but nothing more scuttled out. Quickly the crabs began scutting to get over the side and into water. Mrs. Rowlands was angry and grabbed for the trap, peered inside, upending it, finally reaching her hand in, and letting out a yowl. A large crab grabbed ahold of her sleeve and before Elle even realized what had happened, the man began to laugh; Elle joined him. The comic image of the woman trying to shake a crab off her arm and another crab that seemed more interested in chasing her than making it into the water was too much for them both. Tears rolled down his face, obscuring his vision, so he didn't take in Elle's shocked expression as she looked in the trap again, hardly believing it was empty. All she could think was, *no bones no bones no bones.*

She was overwhelmed with dizziness when she lifted her head. The nauseating stench of crab mingled with Mrs. Rowlands's dazzling white sailor pants, and the wharf spiraled, causing Elle to feel as if she were being hurled out to sea. Her knees buckled and she lost her footing, landing painfully on the boardwalk.

Finally, Mrs. Rowlands returned and again pointed at Elle, who was a good ten feet away from her. The sleeve of Blanche's ripped blouse was wet and stained. When she spoke, a large tortoiseshell comb fell from her hair. She reached for it, cursing, and Elle could have sworn that the man looked from the Rowlands woman to her and gave her a nod. He was smiling, obviously amused at the scene.

"Don't know what happened between you two ladies, but suspect it would be best to shake hands and make up. This Billy, whoever he was, must've been a heck of a guy." He smiled, amused at whatever images he had conjured up.

"Are you cuckoo? This woman has murdered her husband." After Mrs. Rowlands spoke, she must have realized how ridiculous she looked, so she pulled her shoulders back, smoothed her waved bangs, and spoke in as reasonable a tone as she could muster. "Please. Check the boat. I know she has something to hide."

"I'm sorry, ma'am, but I have no more authority to detain this woman. And I got better things to do than get between two women fighting over a man. If you want to arrest her, please do it on your own time. But you'll get no more help from me."

Elle stood, grabbed the hated crab trap and tossed it onto her boat where it landed with a loud thud, the chain lashing over the side. The man raised his eyebrows, obviously impressed at her strength.

"If I may, sir, I'd like to be on my way. Got work to attend to, not like some I know."

There was no denying she had used this same trap to sink Billy's bones. She knew it by the odd shaped wood that made up the bottom. No way those bones could have slipped through any openings. The trap was good and solid enough to hold small, wiry crabs, so someone must have deliberately taken the bones out—especially the long bones that had barely fit in. She tried to push away memories of her hard labor to axe the thighbones in half.

The man was watching her. "G'wan. You're free. So sorry for all the nonsense." He glared at Mrs. Rowlands, who was fussing with her sleeve, tugging at it nervously to hide the rip. Her open mouth showed her dismay at the turn of events and the kindly way the man spoke to Elle.

"Maybe I should act the barbarian like everyone else in this lousy place. Maybe then I'll get some respect." Mrs. Rowlands ripped her sleeve off, threw it onto the wharf, and began tugging at the other sleeve, but it refused to budge. Cat, coming out of nowhere, circled the sleeve delicately, sniffed the air, and began washing his paw.

The man looked warily at the two of them, but said nothing, his eyes empty.

"That sleeve is too well-made to rip easy, ma'am," Elle said, watching Mrs. Rowlands struggle, her voice low. "Got a double seam."

Mrs. Rowlands stood in the sunlight, her bare arm as pale as her blouse, a confused and frustrated expression on her face.

Elle did not bother to hide her contempt. "Billy's gone," she said. "Might as well get used to it." Elle advanced toward her.

Mrs. Rowlands pushed at the air with her palm, a warning to stop Elle from getting any closer.

"Never loved you, nor me. Never loved no one." Elle said, moving to the woman.

Mrs. Rowlands's face was contorted, and tears squeezed their way down her cheeks, bouncing off her starched collar and pinging onto the wharf. Her hands formed fists, as useless as her tears. Elle again remarked to herself that this was how she should feel, in fact, how she might've felt a half-decade or so before. It gave her some sort of weird comfort to know that Billy had his grieving widow, after all, even if it wasn't her.

"Storm got him," she said to the two of them, and she meant it. The man nodded dumbly, in agreement. "Storm got 'em all," he said. "Sure did."

Mrs. Rowlands's face was so full of despair that the man moved in closer and awkwardly patted her on the back. But she was oblivious, her body given over to her sorrow. Elle stood there with her for a few moments, watching, before finally turning to go.

Cat sat silent, waiting on the boat hull, looking out to sea, as if impatient to be off.

38

Elle moved into the small boat carefully, and Cat sat at the prow, letting out a rough murmur as they moved away from the wharf. She turned to watch the bewildered captain and grief stricken Rowlands woman blur and darken as her boat moved farther from the dock. Less than a minute later, they ceased to be real, and it seemed to her that much of life worked this way—an intense moment of drama followed by emptiness, in which she could barely remember the source of the great upheaval. It was much like the waters she travelled upon—a surface that bore no trace of its past.

As the dock receded from view, she took a leisurely pace, paddling, then stopping to talk to Cat, chewing on dried fish and sharing it with him. The trip back to No Name loomed long and hard, the motor refused to turn over, and her arms were sore from paddling and the rough treatment she had received.

No way those bones were at the bottom of water, under the pier. Someone had taken them and placed the empty trap back in the exact position to give her a message. Was it a simple act of kindness? Always something behind any decent act, so what was it she would have to pay out now? And to whom? Was another official on his way to arrest her?

Slowing her pace, Elle tried to remember who had been at the pier since the storm. A few boats always bobbed by the dock, some staying for months on end, though most got hauled up regularly. But things mostly happened in a haphazard fashion. Sometimes a boat would disappear without a word from the owner. Sometimes boats were rented or borrowed for part of the season. Anyhow, it was never her lookout. She knew which boats belonged to the hermit, but he was such a secretive sort that she sometimes spied his skiff upended on his side of the shore, where the trees angled out nicely, affording him a hiding place from which he could see the goings on at the pier. He would rather haul it away than risk coming into contact with people. He was a sneaky one all right, but Elle had always liked the idea that he ruled this place, amused that wealthy patrons held no sway over him. Jimmy, the blue-eyed Bahamian who co-owned the small boat company out of Marathon, took care of most of the boats during high season. He cleaned them, filled them with fuel and supplies, kept his eye on them.

Over the past week, those bones under the pier had haunted Elle, so she had kept careful tabs on who came and went, and only a very few had been by — the Rowlandses, the hermit, workers on the yacht, and Monty. Few boats remained in the water this time of year — hers, the pastor's, and the cottage owner who had registered but failed to show up for the tournament. No one else had been around while Billy's bones hung dangling in the large trap under the wharf. Even still, maneuvering the trap out of the water and getting the bones out was risky and tricky, especially with Elle's house so close to the pier. How could they have known when she would be gone? A few times she had crouched over the side and felt for the thick rope, reassuring herself that it was still there, though she had no way of judging the tension.

Elle realized that the boat had strayed. *Am I more messed up than I think I am?* The second she supposed it, she knew it was true. She had been circling the same small island and now had to fight off the jitters.

Those bones. Someone knew exactly what she had done to Billy, and Elle wished for a safe haven but had nowhere to run, unless she could fetch a price for her small bit of land and concrete. The Rowlandses wanted it and might give her something more just to be rid of the bother.

Damn. Why did that woman have to spot Billy's finger in the chowder and guess the truth about what had happened to Billy? Would she form an unlikely posse with the hermit who must know what had happened? Maybe she would put the squeeze on old man Rowlands to back up her claim against Elle.

Now the fury and tenacity with which Elle had determined to hold onto the land and the house changed places with a hunger to sell it, to be rid of the whole disaster and stake a claim somewhere else. Further up the Keys, maybe. There must be similar places, places that knew nothing of her or of Billy Woodman. Well, nothing quite like No Name, and she let out a breath, visualizing the ragged, stunted trees, the birds of prey overhead, her beloved shoreline.

The channel narrowed and Elle looked around at the large palms, thickening seagrape, and mangrove crowding the land into a narrow finger formation. Cat skimmed the water with his paw but thought better of making an honest swipe. Elle looked over the side into clear water and a gigantic jewfish stopped moving long enough to make a face at her before swimming to Cat's side of the boat. Cat made a show of screeching and cawing then backed down, knowing when he was bested. Elle understood how he felt—all swagger and no substance in the end. A lemon shark slashed through the water but Cat had grown silent, all but his tail disappearing under the loose tarp Elle kept for shelter. She felt the vibration of Cat's purr, but dense mangroves absorbed the sound before it could bounce off the water and into Elle's open ear.

There must be another place up the creek like this, where I could begin again. As soon as she formed the thought, she realized how ridiculous it was. How many widows who could cook and farm would be searching for work? What chance would she have of laying claim on the slender resources of another threadbare territory almost blown away or reduced to tinder in the storm?

No, I must prepare to go far, far away, to a large southern city, where I can find something with what money I have hoarded. Someplace where at least I will be warm.

The channel widened, the vegetation thinned, and Elle realized that she had been heading in the opposite direction of No Name. She had no choice but to stop for fuel or paddle all the way back. Just a few miles to Grassy Key, where Q was bound to have gas on hand, even if only at an inflated price. After struggling with the engine, the sturdy skiff putted its way to the ramshackle wharf at Grassy Key.

A couple of derelict boats were lashed to a severely damaged dock and valiantly held on, as if sensing their fate if they came loose. Elle tied up the skiff and Cat slid deeper under the tarp, his tail disappearing altogether. Tinder and oddments lay heaped in haphazard piles, as if someone had begun an ambitious cleanup but then lost heart, abandoning the project halfway through. Debris was everywhere until getting within fifty feet of Q's store, where it was pristine. How is it possible that he has marigolds and some brazen orange trumpet vine blooming its foolish head off when the rest of the land is stripped of grass and bush? And little more than a week after the storm? One thing it spelled out, loud and clear—he was going to put it to her for gas. He did what he liked, that one.

Elle hauled the rusting tank in and placed it on the counter. "How much for fuel?" She yelled into the back room, where he, no doubt, was dozing.

Silence, so she yelled again. "Anyone about, or should I just help myself?"

"Maybe I have none to spare." He walked forcefully by her and behind the old ornate cash register, festooned with silver curlicues and raised lettering. He rapped his knobby knuckles on the countertop. Raised eyebrows and a set mouth told her to mind the manner in which she spoke to him.

"Your people just about cleaned me out," he said.

"My people? Which people?"

"Old guy. Rough looking. Lives on No Name. Hermit."

"He stopped by?" *What was he doing here?* Elle wondered.

"Not an hour ago. How much fuel you need? Prices dear these days. Things hard to come by."

Elle barely heard him prattle on about the storm and how hard it was to get things. But it didn't mean anything.

Even the hermit had to leave No Name sometime, and it would make sense for him to do whatever he had to do in the outside world during off-season. *No,* she thought, pushing away the fear. *It didn't mean anything.*

"Was he alone?"

"Who?"

"The hermit. Did he have anything with him? Anyone?" Elle had to know.

"A couple of big old crab traps is all. I mind my own damn business. Don't interfere, is my practice. Always has been. Now don't just stand there with your fool mouth agape. All talked out. Get the stuff and be on your way. Best I can do for you is a half tank. Come by later for more."

Elle felt as if someone had shoved her in the chest. *Crab traps? Was he bringing Billy's bones to the Sheriff?* Her shoulders weakened. It was him. It had to be. He knew it all along; he had to. Maybe she could catch up with him.

"When did you say he was here?"

"Less than an hour. Like I said. Right before you."

If I go at full throttle, I can catch up to him. "I need more fuel. I'll pay."

Q began tapping his chin with his long middle finger that was missing its nail.

"Twelve cents a gallon for a full tank. Take 'er or leave 'er."

"Sticks. Toss in some sticks."

"Don't know what you're talking about. More sticks already? Must have plenty of evil to chase out."

"Calm me. They calm me."

He nodded, then blinked his eyes slowly, knowingly, "Gas prices just went up."

"I'll pay separate."

"Not for sale. Told you last time you asked." His ears moved independently from his face and when he turned, they flapped slightly. He was all nose and ears and watery eyes. It was a little like looking on an angry elf.

"Twelve cents a gallon and that's final. G'wan and gecher gas and I'll bring the sticks up front when you're done."

Elle didn't have the energy to protest something that she would only lose in the end. He could've charged her twice that, and she wouldn't have flinched, and he knew it.

He seemed to want to be social when she returned from fueling. The sticks were nowhere in sight, so she was forced to listen about other customers of his while she waited. His eyes were red-rimmed, and thin squalls of smoke escaped from the bib of his overalls whenever he got excited.

He cleared his throat, walked to the open window, and horked up what sounded like a disgusting ball of phlegm. It was so large that she heard it land from inside the store. He continued talking about someone who bought fuel from him. "Think this stuff is near to free. Don't realize the trouble it takes to get it here and the cost too. Make barely enough to get by, but don't never hear me complain." He stuck his face out, daring her to challenge him.

While Elle listened, he seemed to be taking in her appearance, sizing her up. She was desperate to be off but knew how unpredictable he was. Any minute he could toss her out, so she put on a kindly look, whilst feeling nearly demented with panic. This was where fishermen and locals got news and gossip about goings-on, even weather reports. Monty always had interesting news after stopping at Q's.

When he was through speaking, Elle said. "Going to Key West and getting late in the day," she wanted to throw him off in case anyone asked.

"Not my concern," he said

He still refused to take any money outright for the sticks, but she no longer cared.

"Got something for you," he said, his expression kindly.

He went into the back room and quickly returned, trailed by a thin cloud of smoke, holding a cigarette case. Elle supposed he was going to take the sticks out of it but he handed the whole package to her. "Gift," he said. "Don't have need of such fancy ladies' leavings."

She got shoved out the door and into sunlight holding a small, exquisitely carved lady's cigarette case with ten perfectly rolled sticks nestled inside, smooth as long sharks teeth. The top of the case was enameled in a glossy, emerald green, set with small brilliant stones. Elle had never owned anything so fine and quickly stashed it in her neck pouch, before he changed his mind.

She scrambled to the boat, and gunned the sluggish engine as best she could, skidding her way back toward the Lower Keys.

39

She barely made it past the first inlet when she heard a deep rattling. Cat's head was turning like a beast possessed and Elle sensed a heavy gaze upon her before she actually saw him. He was docked, his hands behind his head, watching her. She had to face him. Somehow she knew that he had come for her. The large crab trap was plainly visible on the prow of his boat, his long-fingered, yellow hand patting it rhythmically.

He motioned her over in a fashion that was not unkind. Elle was so weary and had to summon the strength to care about her fate. Her life had come to resemble a purgatory she could not escape. But she would not fall in line with any man or woman's plans for her. Let him do his worst. She was ready. She paddled slowly and he looked away from her face, giving no sign of his mood or plans for her.

"Woman has it out for you, I figure," he said.

"And you?" She asked, her voice low.

He did not answer, only motioned her closer, put his finger to his lips to silence her. From behind, Elle heard a large vessel make its way down the channel, and she wondered if he was setting her up. The hermit must have the dreaded traps that contained every dirty secret she could fathom. Sins she knew would soon be revealed to all. It would almost be a relief to end this sorry struggle. Cat yelled as if to convince her otherwise, and Elle willed her fear away.

No doubt he knew exactly who he was dealing with. That rustling she heard the night she killed Billy, the feeling of being watched, the fresh trail of footprints she had found. They were all his; she was sure now. Certain, too, that he had what remained of Billy's bones to share with all the world.

Sound filled the air and the hermit grabbed the tip of her boat and pulled it into a narrow inlet with surprising strength.

Was it a mistake to be lured here by this man with whom she had shared less than a half-dozen conversations? She noticed his rifle lying across the prow, and he smiled when he saw her spy it. A loud noise split the air between them. They were silent as the sound moved toward them. A large boat moved past, people on deck high above them, carefully negotiating the narrow passageways. A voice rang out. It was Mrs. Rowlands going down the Keys with a pack of helpers.

The hermit nodded at her as if demanding that she choose between two bleak fates. But he was, in many ways, the devil she knew. When he turned to listen, Elle made a grab for the gun, her body jerking back. She had both hands on the rifle, and he used it as a baton to flip her over like a porpoise then drag her onto his boat. She bit into his yellow hand and his whole body seemed to roar, but neither would let go of the gun. The yacht was now almost on top of them, and Elle had to decide whether to fight out this losing battle with someone much stronger than her or yell out for rescuing. Everything in her fought asking Mrs. Rowlands's gang to help her. Maybe her lousy pride would do her in, but she would rather be drowned by a demon than be rescued by that bitch. She grappled for the gun while the boat sailed seamlessly past them, the figures on board looking past them all the while. Elle realized she would have to yell at the top of her strength for them to hear her. She lay hidden in plain sight by a confusion of tall ferns and mud-colored debris.

They briefly stopped struggling, until he heaved the butt end of the rifle into her ribs when she temporarily loosened her grip. Elle fell back into the boat and kicked her legs at the gun, causing him to lose his hold. Cat shrieked and jumped into the hermit's boat and he turned fast enough that Elle grabbed it from him and pulled back the hammer, yelling at him to stop. Her voice rang out so loud that she thought the figures onboard would turn and spot them, and then turn the boat around.

It's Cat—he fears cats. Elle closed one eye and looked at him through the other. "Empty the traps."

"Already done. Before coming here." He stared at Cat, fear in his eyes.

"I said, empty the traps." Cat daintily stepped onto Elle's lap and she nudged him away with her elbow. He was curious and stood with his neck out, sniffing the air, watching while the hermit reached for the traps.

"Move slowly. No need to get spooked."

He upended all three traps and not a single crab emerged. All were empty.

He spoke as he stacked the empty traps. "Deed to the

land is yours if you want it. Lease it twenty years. Mind you, can't ever sell."

Elle felt deflated, not understanding what was going on. She wondered if he knew about Billy or if she had just imagined it. But then why would he want to speak with her? What did he want?

"I bought the land from you until Billy took it," Elle said.

"Not true. I never met the beast. Your husband."

"What you don't know is that it doesn't matter. He sold it from under me."

"I don't reckon that's possible." His olive-yellow eyes burned a hole in her forehead. But she had to make him understand that the Rowlandses had taken over his only access to the wharf and would soon own everything, including No Name Lodge itself.

"Listen to me, Mister. By law, he owns whatever I own. Gives him equal rights to sell—which he did—to the bleeding Rowlandses." Elle gripped the gun for emphasis but the hermit did not appear to notice, or care. Instead, he grinned at her, his eyes slits of yellow. "What if I told you that you never owned nothing? Neither the land or the cistern?"

"I got the deed. Or half of it anyhow. And it's signed and now promised to Blanche Rowlands."

"Call that a deed? Any fool could see it's not real. Guess you're not schooled enough to know the difference. Didn't know if you had it in you to stay and work on No Name. Couldn't risk you up and selling it. But I got something in mind."

"You tricked me."

"Better me than that husband of yours. You gotta serve

someone, Elle. Take your pick—me or the Rowlandses."

The hermit looked from Elle to Cat, and Elle watched an almost imperceptible tremble pass through his body.

"Put down the gun, no more need for that." He struggled to speak as if conversation was the most unpleasant task he could imagine. Elle pulled the gun closer on her lap, keeping it at the ready.

"After the ferry left, I picked up one of the traps. Saw your handiwork."

Elle knew he had a hiding place in the inlet. She'd been spooked by him once before, seen his boat there from time to time, but imagined it to be a secret fishing spot. Men always laid claim to these, even those just visiting for a season. But no, she had been spotted. She hung her head. He had seen what she was capable of, her brutality.

"Saw you in the weeds, too, when you hid the sink, and he went after you."

Was he trying to tell her that it was okay that she killed Billy? That he thought she was justified?

"Foolish man shoulda let you be. You had no choice." His eyes narrowed again. The boat lurched and the crab traps settled. "I came to that slowly. Like you said, I'm in no position to cast stones."

He closed his eyes, pointed his closed fingertips toward the traps as if he expected a volt of electricity to push them away. The trap nearest the side of the boat teetered then fell overboard into the drink without making the smallest splash before disappearing. Neither of them moved. "Then I got to thinkin'. Mostly after I went to the fields and saw the tomatoes, tender as all get out but raising their heads good and determined. I know what it takes to make things grow here, ma'am. I surely do at that." He stared down the channel, seeming to be deep in thought before he continued. "I'm making a bigger field. Kids coming in from Big Pine to clear it out, then spreading high-quality mulch." Elle had never heard him speak at length before and was taken aback by his command of language. "I've got a deal for you, if you've a mind to take it."

"What?"

"Sapodillas."

"Sapodillies? I thought they was a wash?"

"I don't expect that should concern you."

"You expect me to tend 'em, I reckon that makes it my lookout." Elle heard that his father had grown the sweetest, juiciest sapodillas, but somehow either they never made it to market or no one knew what to make of them.

"You could serve them at the lodge. Make a recipe for them."

"You think I have that kind of pull? I'm not that good, Mister." It wasn't the time to tell him of her failure with sapodilla pie. What could you do with that watery fruit? Maybe boil it down, make a better sapodilla pie? Or a drink to mix with booze? Rum-a-dilly? The thought made her bold. "Then I want the land. In my name. This time you be square with me."

"Can't sell it," he answered.

"Don't intend to," she promised.

"I mean I can't."

"Won't is more like it." Elle shook her head.

The hermit sat, his bony knee protruding from a tear in his overalls. He closed his eyes, and when Cat took a swipe at him he leaned back to get away. "One condition. A clause sayin' it reverts back to me if you stay here less than ten years. And if you sell after that, I get to buy it first. And you owe me work."

"Last I checked, slavery ended last century, and I ain't about to trade one master for another."

He picked up the oar and motioned her out, pointing at Cat, who got the message first and hopped back in her boat, followed by Elle. Once she got settled, he began paddling out of the inlet. He had somehow managed to move out ahead of her. On open water, her shoulders released tension.

Before rounding the tip of the finger formation, he yelled, "Build us the best grove this side of the Suwannee. Got to get moving. Planting season upon us. Yes? No?"

She opened her mouth to speak but it was her turn to be mute. Only her head bobbed up and down. Yes. Yes.

Elle gunned the engine then slowed the boat. In the narrow stream, giant palms wove themselves overhead to form a cool canopy. No rush, the lodge party would be waiting when she arrived. She cut the engine, leaned back, took out the cigarette case, and lit one of the sticks for strength. What part of the world would make any sense to her now, after No Name? She was enjoying the second puff, congratulating herself, when she remembered Billy's lost torso with the telltale anchor tattoo. Did the hermit find it and what did he do with it? Did it really matter now? Panic washed over her as she peered into Cat's smug little face then back to the water, preparing for the two-hour trip back home.

For the first time ever, Elle couldn't wait to greet Mrs. Rowlands.

Acknowledgements

To my brother whom I lost this past July 15, 2013. I kept your twisted humor in mind throughout the writing. I hope this makes you laugh from your perch on high.

Gratitude to The Studios Key West. This book is the direct result of the boost of confidence I gained by winning first place for the opening pages of *No Name Key* in the *Writes of Spring* contest sponsored by TSKW in 2012.

Thank you to The Casa Marina Group, a tough and dedicated critique group who have heard every word in this manuscript and helped change many of them. Thank you Mike, Jonathan, Sarah & Michael.

To the Islamorada Librarians who were happy to open archives that held treasures that had not been seen in years, including newspaper articles, pictures and hand-written, first person accounts of how the soldiers were treated by the government when they had to retrieve the bodies of fellow workers after the hurricane.

Thanks also to Key West Historian, Tom Hambright, in the Monroe County Library, Key West, for answering questions about Key West in the Great Depression and how the ferries functioned.

Bill Keogh of Big Pine Kayak Adventures, who didn't flinch when I asked him where he thought the best place to hide a body might be. I have Bill to thank for coming up with Elle's cunning plan.

To first readers Brooks Whitney Phillips, Jonathan Woods, Mike Dennis and Louise Nyeste.

To Harry DeWulf, a brilliant abstract thinker, feminist and editor who specializes in seeing the big picture.

To Laurie Skemp, of http://www.authorsea.com/ the most conscientious editor I have ever encountered, who meticulously weighed the value of every word, caught false notes worked above and beyond, until she thought the manuscript was all it could be. Laurie is the kind of editor a writer dreams of having – combining respect for voice with zero tolerance for poor grammar and an ear for false notes.

Elizabeth Warner and Deborah Linker for showing me the secret place where the manchineel tree grows on No Name Key. After our excursion, it was impossible not to become obsessed with No Name Key, a place of odd and haunting beauty.

To my sister Katie, who shored me up via Skype when the task at hand seemed almost insurmountable.

To Kelly Wheeler who taught me about survival with dignity.

ABOUT THE AUTHOR

Jessica Argyle holds a Master of Arts, specialty Creative Writing from Concordia University in Montreal. She has published numerous short stories in literary magazines. In 2011 she published *Arrest me (Before I Write Again),* a collection of short stories. *No Name Key* is her first novel.

31667404R00174

Made in the USA
Charleston, SC
23 July 2014